BEACH FRONT HUNT

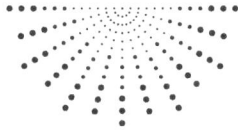

CEECEE JAMES

For my Family 333

And a big thank you to God for giving me a chance to do what I love and write.

CONTENTS

CHAPTER ONE

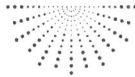

I always loved waking up to warm sunshine peeking through the curtains and the cheerful sound of birds chirping. Like right now, as I extended my arms out with my head on the soft pillow. It only took a nanosecond to realize I should not be seeing the sun stretch across the entire windowsill at this time of the morning.

No! Late again! I couldn't believe it. Every time I had something important to do, I'd lie awake at night with anticipation and stress. Maybe I fell asleep, but the fitful sleep ebbed and flowed, leaving me exhausted.

Similarly, the next morning when the alarm went off, I'd be so deeply asleep the buzzer couldn't wake me. I swear my subconscious sabotaged me.

A glance at the clock confirmed what I already knew, so with some hot words, I bolted from the bed and grabbed my clothes. I jabbed one leg after another into my pants and hopped to the bathroom while trying to yank them up. Not even bothering to button them, I brushed my hair with one hand and my teeth with the other until that didn't work. I had to settle for a crazy bun and clean teeth.

I needed mascara, or else I'd look like I was twelve. That slowed me down. Then it was a mad dash for my shoes and purse. I had a house showing in under an hour.

I ran down the stairs like a horse galloping out of the stall, still trying to button my pants.

"Stella? Is that you?" Mom called from the kitchen.

I still wasn't used to her living with me. I sped into the room where the scent of pancakes and coffee filled the air. Mom stood by the stove, stirring a pile of scrambled eggs in the pan.

Long story short, she'd spent my formative years in prison. In the time since she came to live with me, she'd made me breakfast every single day. I couldn't help but wonder if it wasn't her way of trying to make up for lost time.

"How'd you sleep?" Vani smiled.

"Good. And you?" I searched for my colossal travel mug in the cupboard. Coffee was like mascara. Had to have it.

"Breakfast looks amazing, but, I'm sorry. I'm already late to a showing."

"Oh." Her lip dipped with disappointment, and her spatula stopped moving.

I felt terrible. "Could you save it for me for later? I'll be back in a few hours, and I'd love this for lunch."

She lifted one shoulder. "These won't be good later."

"Maybe call Oscar over. Or Uncle Chris!" I suggested as anxiety started to strangle me. I really had to go.

"You think they'd want to come by?"

"Definitely. Give them a call." I kissed her cheek. "I'll see you later!"

With that, I ran out the door and down the sun-splotched stairs to the car.

I worked for Flamingo Realty, and I was finally getting some respect. It wasn't going to go over well if I was late for Uncle Chris's most important client.

Mr. Hardcastle owned one of the most prominent land development companies in the state. As a real estate mogul, he wanted a private showing to see the Madison Estate. The house wasn't even listed for sale at the moment, making this what was known as a pocket listing, which had fallen into Uncle Chris's lap. The property was worth somewhere in the neighborhood of fourteen million dollars, which would be my biggest deal, if I could cinch it. It was obvious why I couldn't sleep last night.

I shifted the car into gear and stared over my shoulder to back out. Actually, I knew another reason why I'd been so late. My toes curled as I remembered my evening with Carlson. My hunk-a-hunk. I don't even know how I got so lucky to have him.

At least that's how I felt about him today. If someone had asked me last week, I might not have sounded so nice. I'd have been super irritated with him because he left my books out in the rain. So there's that.

At the stoplight, I pulled the mirror down and stared at my reflection. Lovely. It was pretty apparent that I'd just rolled out of bed. My messy bun had slowly slid to the side of my head, looking all too similar to the second scoop on an ice cream cone on a July afternoon. This wasn't going to work.

I put in a call to Mr. Hardcastle. His assistant answered it. How did I know? Because he said, "This is Andy, Mr. Hardcastle's assistant."

"Hi, there," I said. "I'm so sorry, but I'm stuck in traffic right now. I might be a few minutes late."

Andy lowered his voice, which now sounded horror-filled at my predicament. "We've almost arrived. I'll tell you right now he won't be happy. His time is priceless."

I winced. "Got it. I'll be right there."

And I meant it. Except I took a slight detour at the local drug store. Inside, I grabbed a brush and deodorant and a compact of what Maybelline called Racy Face cheekers. After paying for it, I dashed to the bathroom to fix myself up a bit. The pink blush helped to bring me back from looking like an extra from the Walking Dead.

Six-and-a-half minutes later (I know because I was eyeballing my watch the entire time), I'd made it back on the road and headed that way. I sipped coffee, feeling more secure. That's what it was all about, wasn't it? Confidence. Fake it until you make it.

And, today, I was going to fake this. I mean, make it. Either way, I was determined to get this sale.

Luckily, I didn't encounter any real traffic, which would have been pretty uncommon for this sleepy town. Madison Estate was located way up in the mountains in a very regal resort. I drank my coffee, cautioning myself it might be a while before I saw a bathroom as I sped along the road.

The beautiful scenery could be on a picture postcard. Fresh deciduous trees shaded the route this sunny day, with a few fallen leaves littering the pavement. The road hugged the side of the mountain that overlooked a very private lake. The dark water reflected a blue sky as boats dotted its surface. I wished I was out there now, bobbing around. The people who lived here were lucky.

I pulled up to a gate and punched in the code Uncle Chris had messaged me the night before. The gates swung open with nary a sound, and I drove into what felt like another world.

The houses here were gorgeous. I passed mansion after mansion, each one seemingly in competition with the next, what with their pillars and hedges, fountains, and six-car garages. The road slowly led to the top of the mountain where the houses mysteriously remained out of sight down long, manicured driveways.

The road narrowed and started down the other side of the mountain. There were no houses this way, just lush trees that gave way to smaller trees. Sandy mounds prickled with stubby bushes came into view.

I took the next left, onto a road that was fully fenced on both sides. It dead-ended at yet another gate. The rustic gate seemed out of place compared to what I'd recently passed through, and I had to climb out of the car to open it. I shoved the metal frame back and stared from the post. The driveway, all hemmed in with wild shrubbery, curved out of sight. I couldn't see if Mr. Hardcastle had arrived yet.

A breeze came from across the water and felt especially cold. I shivered and hurried back to the car.

The driveway was lengthy. After another couple of minutes, the house finally came into view.

I felt a jolt of surprise. The tiny building looked like a humble pool house compared to the mansions I'd already passed. Weathered gray shakes covered the sides of the house, while green metal made the roof. A stone walkway led from the dirt driveway to a covered porch.

Yet, this was the place. Although the house was small, the value was in the land. And it was right on the beach of this huge lake.

The client's very expensive silver Range Rover was parked in front of me in the narrow driveway. I pulled in behind it and rolled to a stop.

I glanced at my watch and saw that, miraculously, I was only two minutes late. I grabbed my sweater and climbed out.

The waiting vehicle's tinted windows made it impossible to see inside. It felt rude to approach and tap on the window, so I walked over to the large porch and waited.

Nothing happened from the car. Was the client angry over the delay? Maybe preparing to leave?

I turned toward the lake. Well, they wouldn't be escaping easily since I'd essentially blocked them in.

I heard a car door open and then quickly slam shut. I spun back to greet Mr. Hardcastle.

Confusion made me squint my eyes. If it was him, then he was a very thin, young man with bright blue eyes behind wire glasses. His steps were jerky. I wondered if his mannerisms came from being so bean-pole-like. Maybe he felt nervous.

Still, he had a handsome quality about him, and he certainly was polite. "Miss O'Neil?" he called with a quick smile as he approached.

"Yes?" Something was up. He couldn't be Mr. Hardcastle, could he? Were billionaires nervous?

"I'm Andy. I spoke to you on the phone. Mr. Hardcastle would like me to view the house for him."

"Oh, I see." I knew that wasn't necessarily unusual. A lot of people had their assistants vet houses for them. But did they wait in the car while it happened? I glanced at the Range Rover and waved.

I couldn't see a response through the tint, so I turned my attention back to Andy and gave him a big smile. "Well, come on. Let's check it out."

We started the tour, which took no time at all with a house less than two thousand square feet. In the midst of the walk-through, it occurred to me that Mr. Hardcastle might be interested in the house for someone else. But Andy didn't give any details, other than to say the place was nice.

At the door, we said goodbye, and then he buttoned the front of his jacket and headed in his gangly fashion to the Rover.

It was all very anti-climatic. I locked the door and wondered if Mr. Hardcastle wouldn't come out after all.

I didn't have long to wait for my answer. Andy leaped out of the car like a swarm of hornets was hot on his heels. He stared wildly around, his glasses knocked askew. Then he caught my eye and shrieked hysterically. "He's dead!"

CHAPTER TWO

I thought I surely must have heard him wrong. Andy stared at me as though confused himself.

"Who's dead?" I asked rather inanely, my hand frozen on the porch railing. My brain stuttered about three steps behind the information he'd given.

"Mr. Hardcastle! Call the police!" Andy straightened his glasses, still bug-eyed.

I scrambled for my phone from my purse and dialed 911. While it rang, I ran down the steps and over to the Range Rover. "What's the matter? Did you take his pulse? Did he have a heart attack while we were in the house?" The thought made me sick.

Andy backed away from the car. He raked his hands through his hair. "I can't believe this is happening!" He dropped to his heels and made a retching noise.

Maybe there was still time to start CPR. The dark window showed me no more than a shadow, so I yanked the door open.

Immediately I reeled back.

CPR could never restart Mr. Hardcastle's heart. Not when there was a big knife sticking out of the center of his chest. I covered my mouth and tried to breathe. I was so shocked that I didn't realize the operator had been talking to me.

"Hello? What is your emergency? Hello?"

"Hello," I gasped and spun away from the Rover. "I'm calling to report a murder," I whispered the last word.

"Is the suspect still in the area?"

My skin crawled like a sliding snowdrift. I wildly stared about. I realized how terribly isolated Andy and I were. There was no one around for miles. Nearly half of the mountain separated us from any type of civilization.

Where was the murderer?

Oh, no, no, no. This wasn't happening. I stared at the trees and saw one sway.

"Andy!" I hissed, my pulse speeding like my blood consisted of straight caffeine.

The young man had wandered off, both grief and shock stricken, and now crouched by the edge of the driveway with his head in his hands. He moaned loudly. And I knew the murderer could hear him as well.

"Andy!"

He looked back at me with red-rimmed eyes.

Urgently, I waved at him. "Get over here. Come on."

He slowly rose to his feet, making my panic mount. He stumbled over, his hands hanging like ham steaks on the ends of his thin arms. He glanced at the Range Rover, and his skin turned gray.

I grabbed his arm and dragged him back to my car. Wrenching the passenger door open, I half-stuffed him inside. "Get in there. Sit down."

"Ma'am?" asked the operator.

Andy's eyes had a far-away stare that concerned me. Was this shock? What do you do for shock?

"I'm here," I said to the operator. I rattled off the address to the emergency operator and hung up. I realized then that it would be quite a while before anyone arrived. That meant a long, lonely wait for us.

I wasn't happy about that.

I ran to the driver's side and slid into the seat.

Andy moaned. "I can't believe this is happening."

"Me neither." I glanced out the window. "Lock your door."

"What? Why?"

I locked mine. "Because whoever did it is probably still here."

His jaw dropped, and then he scrambled for the door lock. He put on his seatbelt, his hands shaking.

"What are you doing?" I asked.

"What are you doing?" he repeated back, violently gesturing to the steering wheel. "Let's go!"

"We can't leave," I protested.

"What? Why not?"

"They told us to stay here."

"What if that guy comes roaring out of the trees and kills us? Then they find three dead bodies instead of one," he yelled before turning nervously to search out the window again. "There! I think I see someone!"

I stared in that direction. A bush swayed. And did I see shoes? I yanked my seatbelt on as well and jammed my keys into the ignition. "Keep an eye on him! If he comes any closer, I'm outta here."

We gaped at the brush, searching for any movement. Between the light breeze and shifting shadows, I couldn't make out features. Just a frustrating shadow just out of sight.

Andy swallowed, and his Adams' apple joggled in his narrow neck. "What if—" He swallowed again. "What if he has a pistol? Or a rifle?"

Heaven help us, I hadn't thought of that. I scooted down to see out the window better. Goosebumps ran along my arms like an army of ants.

"Why are you saying that, Andy?" I whispered.

"Because isn't that—?" He stabbed his finger in the direction of the trees.

I saw it then. A long rifle. Panicked, my mind went blank, and I didn't think of anything else but getting out of there. I don't even remember turning the key, but as soon as the engine roared, I jerked the gear into reverse and slammed on the gas. My tires spurted gravel as they dug into the dirt.

"Where're we going?" Andy hung on to the hook above the door to hold himself in place as we jostled over the road.

"I'm not sure." I gritted my teeth against the gyrations from the tires. "Call 911 again and let them know we've moved. Maybe we can meet them at the top of the hill."

Andy put the call through. "A gun," he said by way of explanation. "We saw the guy hiding in the woods and had to get out of there."

He described my car as we sped up the hill. Even as the curves fell behind us, I didn't feel comfortable slowing down. The back of my mind said the murderer could be behind me, somehow pop up in some car that he'd hidden along the side of the road.

We reached the top of the hill and now were heading back to the mansion development. The adrenaline faded, and my hands quivered like the last two leaves on an Autumn tree. When I finally pulled to the side of the road, I saw Andy wasn't faring much better.

Luckily, we only had a few minutes to wait before the police arrived. They came roaring up the hill with sirens blaring, red lights flashing.

One cop car edged in front of us and stopped short of my bumper. I saw more cars parked in front of different driveways down the street.

An officer climbed out and approached my door, his hand uncomfortably close to his holster.

I rolled down the window. "I'm the one who called."

"I'm Officer Kent. Can you two please get out of the car so we can talk?"

Andy and I shot each other confused glances. He hesitantly opened his door, and I followed. Another officer approached along the shoulder and waved at Andy to question him.

"What are those cops doing?" I asked Officer Kent and gestured to the cars parked in the driveways.

"They're asking for security footage. We want to see if we can get evidence of what cars recently came through. It's pretty remote out here, so there should only be a few."

I nodded, my mouth dry like I was trying to swallow Saltines. I could've used a sip of my cold coffee right about now.

"How well did you know Mr. Hardcastle?" Officer Kent asked.

"I don't know him at all. My uncle knew him."

"And why were you here?"

"Because we were showing him a pocket listing," I said. The breeze bit through the thin material of my sweater, and I pulled the front closed.

"Who owns this place?"

I shrugged. "I'm not sure. Some corporation, I assume."

"And you know this how?"

16

I stared at him, confused by his questions.

He continued. "Because we just got hold of the owners. And they were quite surprised to hear from us. They had no idea that their house would be shown today. And they have no plans to sell the property. They said you all were trespassing. Interesting, right?"

Officer Kent leaned in close, and I smelled his stale morning breath. He angrily continued, "Why were you really down there? What happened? Don't try to lie. We know more than you think.

CHAPTER THREE

My mouth dropped open so wide I could have caught a hummingbird. Was this officer asking me what I thought he was? Did the man actually believe I killed Mr. Hardcastle?

"You can't be serious," I said. "There's a dagger in his chest. I couldn't do that!" I stared over at wimpy Andy. "And that guy can barely lift a knife to butter his toast. I don't know what's going on here, but somewhere in the mix is a murderer, and he was hiding out at the estate with us."

Officer Kent leaned back, his eyebrows lowering. He squinted in skepticism. "You made a mess of all the evidence. That seems pretty convenient."

"What evidence?" I asked.

"Driving in and out of the driveway. The forensic team wonders if it happened on purpose."

"Did you not hear me tell you we saw someone armed in the woods? What do you think we should have done? Sit there like fish in the barrel?" Shock filled me, quickly outranked by outrage.

"Hold up." He raised his palm as if to make sure I knew to pause. "I wasn't saying that."

"What are you saying, exactly? Because that's what it sounds like, with all this evidence talk. Do you think I wanted to ruin evidence on purpose? I want you to catch the guy! I just didn't want to die."

"I understand. You need to realize we're sifting through everything, trying to get answers ourselves. I'm just trying to do my job, ma'am."

My mouth shriveled at the word "ma'am." Was I really that old?

"So now what?" I asked.

"Well, we're going to continue our investigation. We'll let you know if we have any more questions."

"So…I'm free to go?"

"Yes, ma'am."

There was that darn word again. I rubbed my forehead as I became aware of deep frown lines. Ones that looked like ladder rungs, frowning or not. And why did I care anyway? Someone had died out here, and that was a heck of a lot more important than feeling old.

It didn't matter. I felt sad about Mr. Hardcastle, and I worried about my forehead wrinkles. I guess I could care about more than one thing at once.

The officer dismissed me with a leather-gloved wave. I glanced down the shoulder at Andy. The poor guy wandered aimlessly along the side of the road. He shoved his glasses up his nose as he stared through the gate at a long driveway.

I walked over. He heard me approach and turned his head. "Oh, hello."

"How'd your interview go?"

"Oh." His finger went to those glasses again in what seemed like a habit. "Is that what it was?" His chin dipped as I nodded. "I guess it went okay. They wanted to know why we were there. Did you know the owner says now that the house wasn't even for sale?"

"I heard." I bit my lip. "What made your boss think it was, by the way?"

"He got a phone call. He was told it was a… what do they call it? One of those listings that realtors share before it goes online."

"A pocket listing."

"Yeah." He smiled. "One of those. We were told it was the deal of the century."

"I mean, I get that. There's quite a bit of land involved."

"Yeah." He shivered and rubbed a bony hand along his thin arm. "Much too isolated for me."

"So, do you remember the name of the person who called?"

He shook his head. "Hardcastle got the message privately. He told me to contact his friend, Chris O'Neil at Flamingo Realty."

Of course I knew that part. I groaned as I realized then I still had to call Uncle Chris and give him the news. Could there be anything worse than telling someone his friend died? I bit my lip. Actually, yes, there could. Because the friend had been murdered.

Andy must have misunderstood my groan because he tried to correct himself. "Of course, Mr. Hardcastle wasn't disappointed that you were coming to meet us instead of Mr. O'Neil. He understood that he has employees."

I sighed but didn't bother to clarify that I was his niece. "Yes, that's true. He does. I'm so sorry this happened, Andy. Do you know who might have done it? Does Mr. Hardcastle have any enemies?"

"Funny. That's what the police asked me as well. I mean, anyone who has that kind of money has enemies."

"Anyone...recent?" I pressed.

"What are you, a private detective?" His eyes narrowed irritably.

"Not at all. But my life was in just as much danger as yours. I'd like to know what we might have been facing." And possibly were still facing, I thought but didn't say aloud.

He nodded, accepting that. Rocking back on his heels, he jammed his hands into his sport jacket pockets. "There was someone named Marsh that constantly harassed him. He lost out on a deal Hardcastle bid on. Marsh wasn't happy, let me tell you. It was unfortunate, but sometimes that's the way the ball bounces."

"You think Marsh might have come out here to meet him?" I hated to say the word "kill" but I needed to know the answer. Andy didn't grasp yet that we were basically witnesses. In other words, someone might come looking for us.

"I thought Marsh was in Paris. But that doesn't matter. You realize the killer could have been anyone. When you have that kind of money, you don't do it yourself. You hire someone. That kept Mr. Hardcastle on guard for any kind of attack." He waved his hand as though hitmen were a typical concern in everyday society.

I winced as I realized how depressing that kind of life would be, where anyone could be an enemy. And, sadly, it proved he couldn't have been cautious enough since they got him in the end.

"And you told the police all of that," I asked.

"Of course," he answered impatiently. Huffing a bit, he glanced at his watch. "They're always late."

"Who?" I asked.

"Uber. I'm waiting for a ride. In case you didn't notice, I don't have a car anymore."

I didn't like his sarcastic tone and gave it back to him. "I could have driven you if you'd just asked."

"I'm sorry." He sighed and closed his eyes. I saw how the stress weighed on him. "Mr. Hardcastle got me up early, and I didn't have a chance to eat. Me and lack of food just don't work well together. Then all of this happened. I think I'm just falling apart."

I instantly forgave him. I had plenty of experience of having to run out the door with no food. "You want to cancel your ride, and I'll take you for some food? I know a great burger joint right down the road."

He grinned then, finally putting some color into his pale cheeks. "You serious?"

I nodded. "Yes, of course."

"You got it. I'll even pay."

CHAPTER FOUR

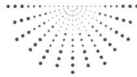

ndy remained quiet as I drove to the restaurant. Now and then, he'd tap his knee with those bony white fingers of his and stare morosely out the window.

I totally understood. I felt kind of tongue-tied myself after the events of the morning.

"Where are we going again?" he asked out of the blue, making me jump.

So, I told him about the Springfield Diner, my favorite restaurant in the whole world. I may have waxed poetic a bit and now had to worry the place would live up to his boosted expectations.

As we pulled in, the red-and-white awnings snapped in the breeze. We barely squeaked into lunchtime. It was eleven-twenty-eight. They started lunch service at eleven-thirty, and the scent of French fries wafted out over the welcome mat, with the Blue-Ribbon Bacon Cheeseburger calling my name.

"This is it?" he asked, a little concerned. He made me uneasy at how his brow wrinkled up as he read the sign.

I realized then he hadn't responded to my descriptions of the food. Alarm hit me that maybe he didn't eat at places that served meat.

Luckily he got out of the car—although he hung on to the door handle a moment longer than necessary—and followed me into the restaurant.

The front door opened as we approached. Mrs. Springfield herself waved her slender arm to welcome us and gave a cheery smile. It never failed to surprise me to see her here at the restaurant, just as active as when she first opened over forty years ago.

"Hello, my love," she said, pressing her little hand on my arm. Her white hair puffed from where she'd pinned it at the back of her head. "How are you today? You look thin! Have you lost weight? Come on, let's get you fed."

I just loved her. I wasn't by any stretch of the imagination thin, but I happily allowed her to lead me to a booth cupped in by a window flower box. Red geraniums filled the container in perfect accompaniment to the yellow sprig in a vase on the table.

She gestured for me to sit, and Andy scooted into the bench across from me.

"I haven't seen you in a while." Wrinkles whiskered out on the sides of her eyes as she studied me. She rubbed my shoulder and squeezed. Her entire frame was about as wide as my thigh, wiry yet surprisingly strong. "You doing okay? I've missed you."

Oh, boy. Was that ever a loaded question. "I'm okay," I lied. I'd now entered the stage of uneasily fearing for my life, but I needn't go into that. Andy arched an eyebrow. I, in turn, ignored him. "Mom's living with me now."

"I heard." She nodded sagely. "And how is that going, love?"

"Surprisingly, very well. We had our adjustment period, but I can honestly say it's been amazing. We're happy." At least this part was true.

"Good. Good. I always say blood finds a way when love is involved. Why, I finally got in contact with my brother who left for the other side of the world nearly twenty years ago. It's been wonderful."

"Really! Where did he live?" I expected to hear her mention a tiny country I knew little about. I about choked when she answered simply, "California."

"You never visited?" I managed to gasp.

"What would a girl like me do in a place like that?"

I had no answer, as her referring to herself as a girl confounded me even more. I dumbly nodded. Luckily, she seemed to take it as agreement because she patted my shoulder again. "I'll send your server right over."

Andy grabbed the menu and scooted his glasses up. I set my menu to the side.

"You not hungry?" he noted.

"I am. I just know what I want." My stomach rumbled in happy expectation. I glanced at him, hoping he didn't notice in the mix of all the surrounding conversations.

"Oh," he said unhappily. His brows lowered as he read the menu.

"Didn't you say you were hungry?" I asked.

He lifted a thin shoulder in a show of indifference.

"Try the bacon bur—" I hadn't even finished before he was furiously shaking his head.

"Are you vegan?" I asked, grabbing up the menu to see what I could find for him.

"No. I just believe in eating healthy."

Lovely. My favorite type of lunch companion, one who judged what I ate.

The waitress came over with two huge glasses of the most lovely ice water I'd ever seen. I realized then how parched I was. I gulped half the glass while Andy reluctantly gave her his order.

She didn't really bother to take mine. Just asked the simple, "Usual?" to which I nodded, causing her to whisk the menus away.

It didn't go well when, a little later, she passed over his fresh pea salad and my fries and burger. His nostrils flared as I swirled a fry in the tartar sauce and popped it in my mouth.

"Mmm," I said, sighing in contentment.

"You know, with the grams of fat that has—"

I held up my hand.

"And the sodium," he added.

This time I sent him the look. The look included flared nostrils and a steely gaze that clearly stated, "Don't mess with my food." This expression has been practiced by every mammal since the beginning of good eating being threatened, and he responded to it right away by returning his attention to his plate.

I took a big bite of my burger and nearly cried as the wonderful deliciousness of cheese, bacon, and dill pickle—and grease. Yes! Grease!—ran over my tongue. I was made not to skip meals. With each bite, I could feel my energy restoring.

"You like that?" Andy's brow rumpled in disgust.

"Want a bite?" I offered the sandwich to him. Actually, I really said something akin to Chewbacca talking, since my mouth was full, but he got the gist and hurriedly shook his head.

"No, thanks," he said with a shiver.

Great. More for me. I took another bite while he fastidiously picked through the salad greens with his fork.

Finally, I was satiated enough to start an intelligent conversation. "So, what do you think happened?"

He stared at me over the top of his glasses, and suddenly his face dropped its judgey look and fell into grief. "I don't know, but I know my life is a mess now. I don't know how I'm going to fix it."

"I'm sorry," I said. I stopped eating.

"This job was a once-in-a-lifetime. He took me everywhere —cruises, vacations around the world. He was talking about me heading up one of his development companies soon." He gave a sarcastic snort. "I doubt Margaret would want that. Now, I'll have to start all over."

"You'll be okay, I just know it. Anyone would want to hire you."

"You think?" He gave a quirky smile and chase a pea.

"I'm positive."

"I might be able to find another job, but I won't find someone like Mr. Hardcastle. He was a tough business man, but, once you got to know him, he had a softer side." He took a deep breath and this time grabbed his napkin and hid his eyes.

I waited for a minute as he took some deep breaths. He looked back at me, his eyes red-rimmed. "Sorry," he whispered.

"It's fine. This is pretty awful."

He nodded.

"Do you have any idea who might have done it? How do you think it happened? "

"Mr. Hardcastle had lots of enemies. But I do know he's been talking a lot with Mr. Tristen Smith. That guy has been calling day and night."

"Who is he?"

"He owns the biggest apartment complex in New York City."

"You mean the Garden?" I licked a fleck of salt from my lip.

"That's one of them. He also owns another two hundred and twenty-two. He's a baller, that's for sure. Not to mention his sleek low profile Mercedes, completely covered in real gold leaf."

My jaw dropped. "What? They do that?"

Andy nodded. "Rich people are weird."

Then I remembered. "What were you saying earlier about Marsh?"

"Marsh and him were in a war over a bankrupt hospital. Hardcastle always wins. As you can imagine, that hasn't gone over well with Marsh. There were some threats made, some scary ones. But these things happen in big money real estate. Anyway, I already told all this to the police."

I nodded and sipped my water. We spent the next little bit with some small talk and finishing our meal. True to his word, he passed his credit card over when the check came.

Of course, I protested, but he wouldn't hear of it.

He glanced at his phone and then anxiously out the window. "Uber says they're outside now."

"Well, thank you for treating me."

"Not a problem. It's the least I can do for a fellow survivor."

We both grinned.

At that moment, the waitress came back with an embarrassed expression on her face. "I'm sorry, sir. This was declined. There might be something wrong with the card. Do you have another?"

His eyes popped open in surprise. Anxiously, he glanced at me as he dug into his pocket for his wallet. "Yeah, of course."

"Here, take mine," I said and slid my card over.

Now it was his turn to protest.

I waved my hand. "Like you said, not a problem, fellow survivor."

The corner of his lip turned up in a faint rendition of a smile. "Fine. Next time it's my treat."

With that, he jumped up, shook my hand. As he walked out the front door, I saw his shoulders slump forward.

I watched him go, feeling sad again.

CHAPTER FIVE

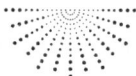

*T*he drive home was not restful at all. My guts knotted in an achy ball, and it had nothing to do with the hamburger.

I knew I had to call Uncle Chris.

I'd delayed it long enough. Biting my thumbnail, I tried to think of how to word the horrible news. I pulled the snag too hard and tasted blood. "Ouch!" I sucked on the hangnail.

I needed to get this done before I destroyed my nails. Squeezing the steering wheel, I took a big breath. Then I pressed the phone button and put in the call.

It rang multiple times. Each peal drained my rapidly weakening resolve. I was about to hang up when he answered. "Yello!"

His sweet, corny greeting about broke my heart. "Hi, Uncle Chris."

"How'd the showing go this morning?"

Well, that removed the problem of how to bring it up. "Not well," I admitted.

"Oh? What happened?"

I swallowed. "Mr. Hardcastle was murdered. At the house."

"What?" he shrieked.

I'd never heard him reach a pitch like that in all the time I'd known him. "Yes. I'm so sorry. I know you guys were friends."

"Are you sure?" he asked, obviously shook.

I thought about the knife and swallowed hard. "Yeah. I'm sure."

Nothing but silence came over the line. I could only imagine what he was thinking. I dreaded telling him how it happened, which of course, was the next question he asked.

I filled him in as quickly as possible and included the man in the woods and how we'd had to run for our lives. I finished with the information about how the cop said that the house hadn't even been for sale.

"You're kidding me," he said again. Obviously, very little had sunk in.

"I'm not kidding, and to be honest I'm in a bit of trouble. The cop really questioned why we were at the house. He accused me of destroying evidence. I need your help to prove Hardcastle asked us to bring him there."

"Okay, I see." His professional voice kicked in. "The request came by email. Let me go find it. I've got it right here. No worries."

There was furious typing in the background and then the dreaded silence began again.

"What's the matter?" I finally asked.

"I can't seem to find it," he admitted.

Oh, no. No. No. No. That couldn't happen. That email was my ticket, my alibi. "Uncle Chris, you have to find it."

"Well, don't worry. Either way, I've got you. I'll simply tell them I read it."

"Will the police believe you, though? You're my uncle. I don't know if family can be each other's alibi," I wailed. I couldn't help it. I didn't want to be in trouble again. I just needed one normal month.

"It'll be fine. You'll see." His overly boisterous tone didn't help my confidence. It was his pulled-over-by-an-officer-for-speeding voice.

I rolled my eyes. "Well, keep looking. I'll keep my fingers crossed," I said.

"I will. Don't you worry."

We hung up, and I gripped the wheel in frustration. Maybe I'd try Oscar. My grandfather always had good advice.

He picked up on the third ring. He was always reliable that way.

"You okay?" he asked. No, hi. No, hello. How did he always know when something was wrong?

"I'm fine, but—"

"But you just came from a murder scene." Oscar finished for me dryly.

I gasped. His intuitive powers were far more extraordinary than I'd ever believed. "How on earth—?"

Again he cut me off. "I have a police scanner. Happened this morning. They have some questions about you."

There were no secrets in this world. "Yes, that's true." I sighed.

"Well, you want to come over?"

At his suggestion, I realize there was nothing more I wanted in the world. "Yes."

"Got the kettle on. Drive safe."

He hung up, true to his usual abrupt self.

Knowing where I was headed already made me feel lighter. I felt prepared to give Mom a heads up.

She answered right away as well. I have to admit, a thin vein of panic still zipped through me when I called her. I worried that one time she wouldn't be there.

"Hi, honey. How'd things go this morning?"

"Horrible," I said and filled her in. She punctuated every one of my sentences with gasps and sad groans.

"I'm so sorry," she said when I finished. "You coming home? Want me to heat you up some food?"

I felt guilty again, thinking of how I'd run out on her breakfast. "No, I'm sorry. I actually am headed to Oscar's."

"Ahh," she said wisely. "Going for a talking moment, I bet."

Her statement caught me off guard. "You know about those?"

"Of course. He has the best listening ear. You hang in there, honey, and relax. I'll be here waiting."

I didn't want her to be trapped around the house for me and told her so.

"Don't be silly," she answered. "I have plenty of projects to do here. One of them is to clean up the space you call a garden out there."

I smiled. I definitely did not have a green thumb.

"Now, what about your father?" she asked. "Have you talked to him? Does he know?"

Dread ran through me. "No," I said, wanting to gnaw my nail again.

"Because he's going to be calling me in a bit."

I breathed heavily through my nose. "Tell him what you think is best," I finally said. I couldn't very well ask her to keep it a secret, not when they were renewing a budding relationship.

"I'll keep it simple and reassure him. Don't you worry."

Just knowing she was going to handle giving him the news felt amazing. "Thanks, Mom. Well, I'm about there. I'll see you later then. Love you."

"Sounds good. Love you, too."

I hung up, sure I was ten pounds lighter. It was nice to have a clan. A tribe. I'd never had one growing up, just Dad and me. I felt rich with all these people now in my life supporting me. Proof you never knew what was around the corner. Funny how you never expected it to be good.

A few minutes later, I turned down the tree-lined road. The ancient trees tunneled the lane, shading it from the hot sun. At the end were two driveways. One led to the Baker Street Bed-and-Breakfast.

The other led to my grandfather's little cottage.

I bumped down the driveway and saw him waiting for me on the front porch, rocking in his chair. A yellow Pomeranian barked madly from his arms. Peanut wasn't in guard-mode though. These were happy, welcome barks. But, regardless of the reason, she modeled a fluffy tornado frenzy and kicked mightily to escape Oscar's arms.

I parked next to the garden shed and climbed out of the car. Oscar gave up trying to contain the little fireball and released her, sending Peanut straight to me. I dropped to my knee with arms stretched out, and she leaped up, nearly knocking the both of us over. I'd hardly regained my balance when the pup was bathing my face with kisses. I knew better than to say anything either to her or Oscar, because she liked to target mouths especially.

Oscar stood in his saggy jeans and a worn t-shirt that advertised some Irish pub with a tipsy winky face. "Well, come on in and get to talking. I don't have all the time in the world left anymore, you know. Besides, I have a bone to pick with you."

CHAPTER SIX

I followed Oscar, and the third board on the old porch creaked in its usual way under our weight. There was a new planter near the front door. Healthy green leaves abundantly spilled over the top. I'd never seen him with plants before.

"What's this?" I asked, touching one of the fragrant fronds.

"Basil," he growled. "Cecelia says it's an herb, and I should have it. I told her I have no use for herby stuff, and she said if I want her to cook for me, I better have fresh basil. So there it is."

I grinned. If anyone could coax some softness and change out of him, it would be Cecelia. She ran the bed-and-breakfast next door, and in the ensuing months, they'd developed a lovely relationship.

His home was tidy, with the worn floorboards shining from the lemon cleaner he loved. "Kills everything!" he'd once told me. His pair of sneakers sat next to the door, crusted with mud. Cecelia must have had him out weeding at her place as well.

Peanut rested her head on my shoulder and warmed my ear with happy pants. The scent of toast and coffee wafted from the kitchen.

"Popped it in when I saw you pull onto the road," Oscar said, flicking the waiting toast out onto a plate. He carried the dish to the table and retrieved the butter and jam from the fridge. Two mugs of steaming coffee already waited at our usual places at the table.

"Sit." He gestured and settled into his seat with a groan. I took the opposite chair, where Peanut immediately stood up on my lap with her tiny paws on the table and stared intently at the toast.

"Bear!" Oscar growled. "Manners, for Pete's sake."

Peanut scooted down. She glanced at the toast and back at Oscar and gave a sharp yip.

"That's better." Oscar tore off a corner. He tossed it to the floor. This caused Peanut to propel herself from my lap like a jet, in the process digging very sharp nails into my thigh.

"Oww! Next time warn me." I rubbed my skin.

Oscar looked chagrined. "She said please."

I smiled. That she did.

"So, what's the bone you have to pick with me?" I asked.

He glanced at the clock on the wall. "This all happened hours ago. What took you so long?" he asked, cupping his mug in a calloused hand.

I sipped my coffee and closed my eyes, letting the stress wash away in the presence of the safety of family. "Sorry. I had lunch after the police questioning. Long story short, when I arrived to show the house, Mr. Hardcastle wouldn't leave the car. Instead, he sent his assistant to view the house for him. When Andy and I finished, the man was dead."

"And you didn't hear anything?"

I sadly shook my head. I then shared all the police questions, stressing how they'd insinuated I'd purposely tried to cover up evidence.

"Hmph," he said angrily. "Makes no sense why they'd think that. Well, they'll find him soon. Or the evidence."

"The killer?" I clarified.

Oscar gave a stiff nod, his eyebrows bristling over his glasses. "That's right. They'll be combing the woods right now, looking for the guy with the rifle. They'll get a bite on him, you'll see."

At the word "bite," Peanut barked again. Oscar rolled his eyes. "I teach you one word," he muttered and tore off another corner and passed it down.

I finished my coffee. "Well, I better get back home," I said, standing up.

"You're not eating the toast?"

"Peanut can have it."

He glared at me.

"I mean Bear," I said, my hands held up in compliance.

"That's what I thought you said." He gave me the stink eye, but I couldn't stop my smile. I carried my mug to the sink and gave him a quick hug before leaving for the car.

As I pulled out of his driveway, I realized I still wasn't quite ready to go home. I could head to the Flamingo Realty office, but did I really want to be around Uncle Chris right now? Especially with the stress of not knowing where the original emails had disappeared to. It made me feel out of control, and I hated that feeling.

There was only one other person I wanted to see who could make me feel as good as family.

Carlson.

Since he was on duty, I knew I couldn't call him, so I sent him a quick text. — **You busy?**

He usually got back to me pretty fast, and today was no different. — **Yeah. Worrying about you.**

I bit my lip. — **Oh, you heard?**

— **Heard? I've been pacing like a maniac, waiting for you to call.**

Waiting? — **You didn't have to wait. You could have called me.**

— **I knew you needed some time to process. How bout I call you now?**

For him to understand that about me showed me he really knew me. And, even better, accepted me the way I was. He didn't have to ask me twice. I wasn't going to leave him in suspense any longer. — **Yes!**

My phone rang in the next instant. "Hello!" I answered, the corners of my lips already turning up into a smile.

"Gurrl," he drawled out.

"I swear, I had nothing to do with any of it," I blurted, already hearing his unasked questions stabbing me in that one word. "I merely showed a house. It was supposed to earn me a huge commission. My biggest one yet!"

"Aren't you kind of new to the business?"

"Yes," I answered a little hotly. What was that supposed to mean?

"Don't you think it's a little odd that someone with that kind of money would ask for you? I mean, I think you're pretty amazing, Hollywood, but not everyone knows you like I do."

I started to answer when I realized how much his question made sense. Why wouldn't Hardcastle want someone with more experience? How had he even known my name?

"I'm not sure. The request came through to my uncle. What's even weirder is the message his company sent is gone."

"They sent it critically then," Carlson said dryly.

"What's that mean?"

"It's a computer program that erases the message after a certain amount of time passes. Why would they go through all that trouble?"

Carlson knew why. He waited for it to occur to me.

"Because they were setting up his murder. But why me?" My thumbnail called to me and I made a fist to hide it.

"Because someone thinks you're the perfect Patsy, maybe. Or something else is going on." I heard rustling and then the pop of a soda can. He took a sip.

"Well, I think I saw the guy. He hid in the woods, spying on us."

"What did you see?" His voice rose with concern.

"Movement and a rifle. That's why I ended up taking off. I thought he might come after us next."

"How tall was the person? What kind of rifle? Did you see a scope?"

I had to answer no to all his questions. "You can't believe how dark it was in those trees. And I didn't want to stick around and give him a nice still target. You have no idea how isolated the place is. Honestly, I'm thankful I wasn't flying on adrenaline so high that I couldn't drive."

He sucked in a deep breath. "You did good, Hollywood. It's a terrifying situation. I know the area, at least on the other side of the lake. My uncle and I used to hunt out there. You're right. There's nothing around for miles and miles."

I shivered, remembering how alone I'd felt.

"But I can't say I'm not still worried. Whoever was out there got a good look at you, your car, and your license plate. I need you to do me a favor. Stay safe, and stay aware of your surroundings. You see anything funny, you call me, or you call 911. Got it?"

I nodded. "I'm headed home now. Don't worry."

"I know you're a tough cookie, Stella. But telling me not to worry right about now is like telling a southern woman not to serve sweet tea." He sighed. "It just isn't happening."

CHAPTER SEVEN

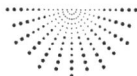

*a*s I drove home, I thought about how much my life had changed since I moved from Seattle to Pennsylvania. Honestly, I still had goosebumps when I remembered my first night here. The moving truck had gotten lost, and I'd wondered what in the world I'd done to move out here.

And I almost left.

I felt sick with gratitude that I hadn't given in to temptation and turned tail to run. That remained a pinnacle moment for me. The consequences of that choice were more than I could imagine. Terrifyingly, I would have missed out on meeting my mom.

I pulled into the driveway and saw, true to her word, she'd dragged out the hose and now was spraying the garden. A straw hat from who knows where perched crookedly on her head. She waved when she heard me and turned off the water.

I had strange expectations of what she would be like when she first came here. She was so soft-spoken and bird-like, I'd been sure she'd be timid and the conversation forced. Instead, on that very first day she'd bounced up the porch steps and examined the foyer with a huge smile.

"You did all of these repairs? It's gorgeous!" She'd turned from gushing to grab my hands. "Honey, it's beautiful!"

I loved that she loved my home. Since she'd lived there, the atmosphere seemed even more swirled with cinnamony-homeyness. It tickled me that we appreciated the same things. And I especially was grateful for the gift of time we now had to learn about each other.

"Hi, Mom," I called after I parked.

"Hi, sweetie. How are you coping? Your talk with Oscar go well?"

"He helped. He always does."

"Aw." She walked over as she wiped her hands on her jeans. There was a moment of awkwardness, and then she pulled me in for a hug.

I'm not a touchy-feely person, but I've got to say, the hug felt nice.

"I'm just glad you got out of there safely. That had to be so scary. Did you hear any news?"

"No. Nothing at all. How did the talk go with Dad?"

She made a face. "It didn't start wonderful. He insisted that you *promised* you'd quit finding dead bodies. I assured him it was not your fault, and you were okay."

"Oh, geez."

"While you were gone, you got this phone message." She found a paper from her back pocket and handed it over to me. In meticulous cursive writing, she'd taken the information from Uncle Chris. It said, "Does the name Tristen Smith mean anything to you?"

"Tristen... it sounds familiar." I frowned. The stress had me all addled. "Did Uncle Chris say anything else?"

"That was all. He said he'd be calling you later."

Hm. I headed into the house and went straight to my desk for my laptop to look this Tristen guy up. Mom followed me inside, leaving me to putter around in the kitchen.

Uncle Chris wouldn't have brought up a name unless it meant something important. I logged into my Flamingo Realty account to see if he was someone we'd previously done business with. That, however, came up as a dead end.

I loaded a social media site and typed his name in the search bar. Seriously, time and time again, this proved to be the fastest way to dig up information on a person. In the past, I've even typed unknown phone numbers and found the caller that way.

A profile did come up, someone way out of my pay bracket. It was of a gold Mercedes. I remembered then that Andy had mentioned him.

"How's it going? Did you find anything?" Mom asked, entering the room. She carried two cups of tea. At least, I'd thought it was tea, but upon receiving the mug, I saw cocoa with mini marshmallows. It made me smile. It was these little things she did as if getting a redo from my childhood.

I took a sip and relished the rich chocolate. Maybe it was a redo for me too.

"I found him." I turned the laptop toward her.

Mom brushed her hair behind her ear as she leaned over to look. "Oh." She nodded wisely and took a sip of her cocoa. "Tristen Smith. Yeah, I've heard of him." It was hard to see her as wise with the chocolate mustache.

"You have?" Surprise flitted through me. How did she know him and I didn't?

"We did get TV in the big house, you know. Sure, I saw him."

"What do you know about him? And why do you think Uncle Chris asked me that?" I quickly sent him a text asking just that.

"Well, I heard he was buying out on the east coast."

"Really? How did you hear that?"

"On one of those real estate shows. He's gobbling up a lot of spare land. Supposedly he has a lot of foreign clients he shops for."

I rubbed my neck as I studied his profile. A PA person ran the profile page. It hosted flashy pictures taken with photoshop on blast. Tristen was actually a handsome man with dark hair and blazing blue eyes. In each photo, Tristen hosted tan, expensive clothes, and perfect chicklet teeth. There were zero personal posts.

I checked for Tristen on another social media site. This time I saw he'd recently paid a visit to our state. He'd been tagged in a photo at the most expensive restaurant in Philadelphia.

I clicked the picture to examine it further. My jaw dropped when I saw his companion.

Mr. Hardcastle.

Whoa. The time on the post shocked me even more. The picture had been taken only forty-eight hours ago. The two men appeared friendly enough in the photograph. Tristen sat with a drink in front of him, hands linked behind his head in a stretched, relaxed way. Mr. Hardcastle stood awkwardly as though he'd just rose to his feet to leave. Both of them wore amiable expressions of one used to being snapped in public.

"Check this out." I pointed it to Mom. "That's the man who died today. And that's Tristen."

"My goodness," she said. "They were quite chummy."

"Maybe too chummy. You think Tristen could be a suspect? Maybe the answer boiled down to something as simple as a war between two competitive land moguls."

"I've heard weaker motives than that for murder," she answered sadly.

I realized she probably had. I wanted to get excited, but something stuck in my logic. "Why would he kill Hardcastle at Madison Estate? Not to mention the police said the property wasn't even for sale. I wish I knew who gave Mr. Hardcastle the heads up to go there in the first place."

I checked my phone to see if Uncle Chris had responded. There was nothing. I thought about sending Officer Kent this tidbit about the photograph, but I figured the cops had to be searching through all the same things.

I needed to get to the bottom of why Uncle Chris asked me about Tristen in the first place. And why had those two men met at the restaurant?

Sighing, I pushed the computer away. The two men were probably best friends or something.

I glanced at Mom. "Hey, you got a little something there."

She laughed. "You do, too."

I followed her to the bathroom where, sure enough, we had twin mustaches. I couldn't help it. I had to take a selfie for posterity, with our arms around each other.

CHAPTER EIGHT

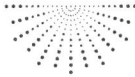

ncle Chris didn't get back right away to me. Apparently, after several meetings the next day with the clients, he had a surprise one with the city council to discuss the purchase of land for a new stadium. So, it wasn't until late that night that I finally heard back from him. And that was a simple text explaining he'd see me first thing in the morning.

The next day, he arrived at Flamingo Realty about thirty minutes after I did, dressed in clothes that appeared as if they'd been dragged behind a truck before he put them on. His face was red and beaded with sweat.

"Stella, I'm glad you're here," he said upon spotting me.

"I'm glad *you're* here," I repeated. "I've been waiting impatiently to learn what you've found out."

"I'm sorry. Things have been crazy around here. After my meetings, I had to take a little emergency business trip. I only just got back this morning."

"Oh? Where'd you go?" And I'd thought the meeting with the city council was a surprise.

He glanced across the room at our new receptionist and lowered his voice. "Grab me a coffee and meet me in my office, okay? I need to clean up a bit."

He walked toward the restroom. I realized then he must have slept in his clothes.

I went to our breakfast bar, always well stocked in the morning, and poured two cups of coffee. On second thought, I added a doughnut across the lids of both and, carefully balancing the pile, I carried them into his office.

He still hadn't returned. I deposited the cups on his desk and idly glanced over his workspace, wondering if something was out that could explain why he'd been called to an emergency.

Everything seemed fairly ordinary, at least for him. Stacks of folders that leaned in a threatening way, two old coffee cups, a fast food container that had almost made it in the trashcan. I was about to sit down when I spotted a note. *"Marsh offered to renegotiate."*

I heard the bathroom door close and hurriedly sat in the chair across from the desk. A few moments later, Uncle Chris came in.

He'd lost quite a bit of weight over the last few months, but he still remained a big man. He must have had a spare set of clothes tucked around here somewhere, because he now wore a new shirt. His wet hair and red face attested to a good scrubbing.

His eyes lit up at the coffee, and he grabbed it before he'd even sat. The chair squeaked alarmingly under his weight. Unperturbed, he took a big swig. "Mm. Thank you." He smacked his lips appreciatively.

"So?" I asked, leaning forward. I'd forgotten all about my doughnut and snatched it up.

"So, after your little adventure yesterday—"

"I'd hardly call it an adventure," I huffed around a crumbly bite.

"Whatever. After Mr. Hardcastle's death yesterday I was quite concerned to find the emails asking that we show him the Madison Estate had disappeared from my computer."

I nodded and took another bite.

"So, I called this guy I know who's amazing with computers. Scott virtually connected with mine and remotely did a complete search. And what he discovered was the reason for my trip."

"What was that?"

"I'll get to that. First, what do you know of Dennis Clark?"

I shook my head. "Never heard of him. Is he related somehow to the Tristen guy you were asking me about yesterday?"

"Dennis is a famous, or maybe the term is infamous, Australian hacker. Ransomware has nothing on him. Apparently, when he sends his nasty little program, he leaves an Easter egg. He leaves it in a spot where no one but an expert could find it. Lucky for me, my friend is an expert."

"What's the Easter egg?"

"It's a little winky face. Guy thinks he's a comedian." He took another swig and then stared at me thoughtfully. "And we found one on my hard drive."

"Oh, wow. So who do you think Dennis is working with?"

"Dennis keeps his associate list pretty tight-lipped, as you can imagine. But I pulled in a favor and yesterday met with the hotel general manager. He confirmed to me that Dennis Clark recently flew into town and stayed at the hotel under an alias." He stretched back in the chair with his fingers laced behind his head.

"How did you get the general manager to confess that?"

"Like I said. I pulled in a favor. The guy owed me because I held a realty convention at his hotel, which had it booked solid for a week, and now it's permanently on the realty conference cycle. He wants to keep me on his good side."

"So, is the manager going to share that with the police?" I popped the last bite in.

"I asked him to, but I don't have high hopes. And I can't make him. In the end, with the alias, it would be my word against his. This little bit of information might be just for us, I guess. At least until I can get a few more pieces."

"What can I do to help?" I asked, leaning forward.

"Help?" His eyebrows shot up in surprise and then lowered forcefully. "You aren't helping no one. No, I need you to hold down the fort and stay safe. Keep your eye out for strangers."

I narrowed my eyes. He sounded suspiciously like Carlson. "Did Carlson call you?"

"We might have had a conversation." He shrugged casually. Then he sent me a steely glare. "But I'm serious. You need to stay safe."

"Pish. Safety is my middle name." I rolled my eyes. "Now, what about Tristen?"

"The manager had one more tidbit. He mentioned there was a rumor of Dennis being out at the Appaloosa Resort."

"Yeah? So?" I had no idea where this was. Some sort of dude ranch, maybe?

"That's Tristen Smith's place. He purchased it back when he was in his twenties."

I raised my eyebrows. "Interesting. I heard Tristen had a real-estate show on TV. And there's a picture of both him and Hardcastle at the Oyster Bar restaurant."

Uncle Chris nodded. "There you go. That's why I took that outing yesterday in the direction of Appaloosa Resort to see if I could get more information, private like."

"Anything?"

"There are rumors that Tristen had taken an interest in Hardcastle's private life, snooping around and such. Keeping tabs on Hardcastle's whereabouts. But I'm also not sure why that billionaire would care two hoots over what Hardcastle does or what he buys."

"For all that snooping, there's a photo of them having a meal with each other."

Uncle Chris shrugged. "Maybe. My sources said they weren't at the restaurant together, though. Despite what the picture says."

CHAPTER NINE

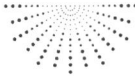

I leaned forward in the chair, confused. "The picture sure makes it appear like Hardcastle and Tristen are together." I brought the photo up on my phone and held it toward him. "See?"

He studied it for a second, and then lifted his shoulders. "I'm not sure. To me, it looks like Hardcastle photobombed Tristen. He's standing."

I stared at it again. "Maybe. Did your computer guy ever find the emails asking that we show Hardcastle the property?"

Uncle Chris shook his head. "They're gone. Including the bit where Hardcastle specifically asked for you. How about you? Did you ask Andy about who had alerted his boss to the deal?"

"He doesn't know, either."

"How's Andy doing, anyway?"

"He was pretty shaken." I cringed, remembering his shrieks. "Poor guy. I should check on him today."

"Yeah, why don't you do that. And prod him again who could have put Hardcastle on this property."

I circled the coffee lid with my fingertip, in the process, wiping off a tiny droplet. "Don't you think the police will ask him?"

"Probably, but they might not get back to us with the information. I'd like to know myself."

"All right. I will. In the meantime, I've got some contracts to go over today."

"You get on that. I'll talk with you later, then. Try and have a mellow day."

I laughed and headed out into the main office, tossing my cup in the trashcan along the way.

Kari rushed through the front door with her arms full. She juggled Amazon boxes, a purse, a jacket, and a travel mug. Her eyes were wide and wild.

"Here, let me help you," I said and ran to take the two top boxes.

"Holy Heavens, what a morning."

I smiled. Kari's hair reminded me of a mad scientist's. She really must've been having a day. "What's going on?"

"Late! Frazzled! Colby had a science project due, and Christina needed a permission slip signed that she somehow lost. So we had to tear the house apart, trying to find it. At the last minute, Joe lost his car keys. Guess where we found them." Her face remained stoic.

"Where?"

"In the freezer. He says he got himself some ice cream last night when he got home and must have stuck them in there. Who does that?"

I laughed. "What did you do for a science experiment?"

"I almost sent Colby with my houseplant to show the results of a living in a house with constant chaos and sporadic watering, but he didn't want that. So instead he took in a jar filled with vinegar and a raw egg."

I must have looked blank because she explained in a rush. "The egg turns into rubber after a few days, you know." Concern flickered over her face. "But more importantly, how are you? What a day yesterday, huh?"

I snorted. "That's putting it lightly."

"Ugh. What are you doing now?" She had out her phone and checked for messages.

"Going over some contracts to submit. Trying not to obsess over what happened."

"Aw, I hear you. I have a few new listings to get ready, but maybe we can do lunch later. I'd love to be able to treat you and get a chance to catch up."

My hesitation must have showed on my face because she immediately continued, "I'm serious. I know you hate for people to pay for your meal, but you deserve it after all you've been through."

I smiled. She was so sweet. "If you're sure."

"If I'm sure? Of course, I'm sure. It's a date then!"

Kari bustled over to the breakfast table and caught a glimpse of her reflection in the glass-covered picture above the table. "Good grief! My hair! It looks like a wild animal licked something off my head," she said, wide-eyed. She frantically tried to pat it down while turning to me. "You just let me walk around like this?"

"Fashion statement," I said with a grin.

She rolled her eyes. Somewhat satisfied with what the glass showed her, she filled a mug with coffee. She paused before the donuts, even going so far as putting on a pair of reading glasses. With a sigh of regret, she left them behind and headed to her computer.

I clicked my computer screen, waking it up, and got to work on my emails. An unopened message with a red flag in the corner rested at the bottom of the list. Curious, I clicked it.

Immediately, a little PacMan symbol appeared at the top left corner of my screen. It started gobbling to the right, and as it advanced, it left a streak of black. Not my screen saver, no icons.

I hit the return button. I couldn't get it to stop. I hit the escape button. If anything, it seemed to speed the hungry icon up. "Oh, no. No! No! No!" I hit the delete button. "Kari!" I yelled.

"Hm?" she said, staring up over her screen, her eyes magnified behind the glasses.

Half the screen was already gone. "Emergency! I need help! Uncle Chris!"

That spurred some movement. Kari jumped from her seat. "What's the matter?"

The door to Uncle Chris's office slammed open. "Emergency?"

"Yes!" I yelled frantically. "I clicked something, and now my screen is disappearing."

Kari leaned over my shoulder and feverishly pressed keys. Nothing happened. By now, Uncle Chris was there, staring at the screen. He went around back and yanked the power cord.

Immediately the screen went black.

"What happened?" he asked, holding the power cord like a dead mouse tail.

"I clicked my emails. There was a flag at the bottom. It wasn't even an attachment." I tried to defend myself.

"With the price of the virus software, that should never happen even if it was a Trojan horse." Frowning, he rubbed his neck with a beefy hand. "Guess I need to give Scott a call again."

He walked away, dialing his cell phone.

Kari stared at me, glasses on her head and eyelashes darkly fringed with mascara. "That was nuts."

"I can't even believe it."

"And so sinister with the PacMan, like it was a joke."

I shook my head.

A second later, Uncle Chris returned. "Well, I'm going to need you to bring the tower down to him, if you don't mind. Scott wants to look it over."

"Why can't he do it remotely like he did yours?" I asked.

"He doesn't want to chance me plugging it in again. Can you leave right now?"

"Sure. Where's he at?"

"Lochsloy. It's a drive, over an hour away. You sure you don't mind?"

"That was my whole morning right there," I said, pointing to the machine. "Disappeared right into PacMan's mouth. Now, what am I going to do?"

"Let me know when you're back, and we'll meet for lunch still," Kari whispered, squeezing my arm. She returned to her desk while Uncle Chris disconnected all the wires. Then, he heaved the tower from the cabinet and set it with a bang on the desk. I refilled my coffee cup—today, I felt heartburn was worth the risk. I needed it. I carried my purse and coffee to the car and came back for the tower.

Uncle Chris held the door open. "I texted the address and phone number to you."

"Thank you," I said, shifting the heavy machine in my arms as the metal started to cut into my hands. He followed me and opened the back passenger door. I belted the tower in for extra protection.

Before I left, Uncle Chris gave me a hug.

"Aw," I said. "I promise I'll drive safe. Don't worry."

"You can't say that after taking me to Oscar's the other day. Those stop signs aren't suggestions, you know."

I rolled my eyes. "You used to race cars. Don't even go there."

He laughed. "This is what I get for telling you my old stories." His face grew serious. "Anyway, I just have a bad feeling about the virus. The way you said it happened, it's too close to what happened to me yesterday with my email."

"Okay, so maybe it's the same person. So what?"

"How does he know your email address? Why does he care about you at all?"

Those were questions I'd be repeating to myself for the entire drive.

CHAPTER TEN

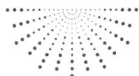

*O*nce on the road, I spun the radio volume like it was the Wheel of Fortune dial and blasted music all the way to Lochsloy. Of course, I sang along at the top of my lungs. Something about the bass vibrations and hearing those perfect notes set my teenage Pop Star-side free.

All was fine and well until I pulled up to the stoplight and glanced to my left. I saw I'd been caught singing by another driver. I sheepishly smiled and waved before stepping on the gas and belting out the chorus again.

The GPS led me to what appeared to be an abandoned warehouse factory. It was a little creepy driving through the empty parking lots in search of the address. Finally, I spotted the computer repair shop tucked under a metal awning beside an old tire shop. How on earth had Uncle Chris found this guy?

I parked the car, climbed out, and slid on my sunglasses. I studied the area. The only other vehicle around happened to be a beat-up little Toyota truck covered in rust spots like it had impetigo. I checked the address for confirmation and then turned to haul the tower from the backseat. That thing was massive and grew heavier as I carried it. It took a little balancing on my knee, but I wrestled the door open and shimmied inside with the door bumping me in the back.

The office space was just a sliver of the entire building. And empty of human life, it seemed. Lovely.

"Hello?" I called, walking over to the counter and dumping my load off with a heavy bang. "Anyone here?"

Scrambling sounds came from a back area, and then a young man appeared through the door. He wore thick glasses and had premature balding. But he had a nice smile, and his eyes were warm and friendly. "Hi, there. You with Chris O'Neil?"

"Yep. That's my uncle. And you're Scott?"

"That would be me. And this is the trouble machine, hm?" His eyes sparkled when he saw it. His interest perked like it was an extra-large pizza. He spun the tower around to examine the back.

"That's right," I answered. "You think you can fix it?"

"We'll find out. However, I've never had a machine I couldn't fix." He slid a clipboard across the counter. "Just fill that form. I'll get right on it after I finish up with another client."

"Great! Thanks!" I found a pen and quickly got to writing. Scott carried the tower back to wherever he'd come from. "Talk to you later!" I called to his retreating back.

"You'll hear from me soon," he assured me without looking back.

I returned to my car, where I texted Kari to see if she'd be ready for lunch in an hour. She responded with a thumbs up and the suggestion of the new little Italian restaurant in town. I responded that I'd see her there and then headed out.

A few minutes later, with the radio blaring and me singing again, the phone rang. Thinking it was kind of fast for the computer guy, I lowered the volume and answered, "Hello?"

"Stella, how are you?" Mrs. Carmichael asked. She owned the house I rented. She'd retired some time ago but still glided through life with an elegant, youthful air, always dressed impeccably in either white linen pants freshly ironed or a sublime skirt and silk blouse.

"Hi, Mrs. Carmichael. How are you?"

"I'm good. It's been a while since we've connected. I wanted to see how things were going with you and your mom."

She knew how rough it had been when I'd flown to Florida. Not many people have their mom kidnapped right before meeting them for the first time in over twenty years.

"We are slowly recovering," I admitted. "But it's kind of nice because we went through that crisis together. We understand each other's feelings."

"Very true. Many people bond over trauma. You both are survivors and now thriving. I'm proud of you."

I respected Mrs. Carmichael so much that her words hit me in a soft spot. My eyes stung, and I had to blink hard. "Thank you. We really are doing well. She saw a counselor for a while, and I think that helped too."

"And what about you? Do you have someone to talk with?"

I thought about Carlson, Oscar, Uncle Chris, and Kari. "Actually, I have a lot. More than I could have ever dreamed of even a few years ago."

"That's wonderful. I'm so happy to hear this. And you have me as well, if you need someone else. Unfortunately, I have something to share with you. I don't want to throw a wrench in your life when things are going so well, but I'm afraid I must."

"What is it?" Something about her tone was off. Fear prickled my skin.

"It seems I have to sell that little house soon. I'll try to delay it for as long as possible, but there it is."

Sell my house? "Why, what's happened?"

"My brother has come back into the picture. He's contested the will, saying it wasn't fair that I got the house, and he wants it sold. Unfortunately it looks like he has a leg to stand on, and I've been told it has to go."

"Can you just buy him out?"

"I looked into that. He's being disgustingly vindictive and won't allow it. He's sadly forcing my hand."

I closed my eyes. I loved my little house. This was the worst news ever. But if I felt horrible, I could only imagine how Mrs. Carmichael felt. This had once been her childhood home.

"And the thing is, it's not like he even needs the funds." Her voice dropped bitterly. "He has more liquid income than several people on the Forbes list."

"Then why is he doing this?"

"He hated my mom and wants nothing around that has her name on it. I think he wants to hurt me. I was her favorite."

"He didn't get along with her?"

"My mom was his stepmom. He's always dealt with bitter memories about our childhood. He tormented her for years after our dad died."

I swallowed hard. It amazed me to realize that I wasn't alone with having crazy family dynamics. So many other people did as well, even though their lives looked picture perfect on the outside. It was a little shocking to get a view behind the looking glass.

"I'm so sorry, Mrs. Carmichael."

"Well, there it is. Life is crazy. In the end we can't take anything with us and can only leave the memory of loving well. I just wish we could learn not to hurt each other along the journey."

"That would be good," I agreed.

"Anyway, dear. I'll fill you in when I know more. As I said, I'm going as slow as possible, and my attorney is doing his best to stall. I'm just not sure how much longer we can, so I want you to be prepared. We'll talk soon."

We said goodbye. I gripped the steering wheel tightly. I had a wild thought that I wished I could buy the little house, but my bank account barely reflected enough for a nice meal out, let alone a down payment. Now I needed to find another home for my new little family.

CHAPTER ELEVEN

I groaned when I saw how packed the parking lot was at the Italian restaurant. In fact, the feeling turned slightly panicky when I couldn't find a spare spot. Which yo-yoed into me cheering when I finally found one, only to plummet as I walked inside and saw the overflow booths filled with people all waiting to be seated.

I sent Kari a text to let her know I'd arrived. Eventually, a server with a perfunctory smile walked over to me.

"Just one?" She grabbed a menu.

"Two. My friend will be here soon."

She snagged another. "Right this way."

I followed her through the crowded restaurant to a booth in the way back. I loved booths, so I was overjoyed. The sweet ambiance of the thriving business was bolstered by its red upholstery, copper lights overhead, and a beautiful mural of vine country over one wall. Garlic and fresh bread filled the air with their delicious scents.

The waitress asked what I'd like to drink, and I ordered two waters and two iced teas.

I'd hardly looked over the menu when Kari showed up. Her hair might have been in better form, but she still exuded chaos.

"Hey, lady," she said breathlessly as she slid into the other side. She dropped her bag with a thump. "Holy buckets, what a day."

"It hasn't mellowed out?" I sipped my tea. My mouth puckered at the lack of sugar which I hurriedly corrected.

"Mellowed, ha! Right after you left, the school called. Colby dropped his egg. He's grounded for two weeks."

"Aw. Just for dropping it?"

She pressed her lips. "It landed on his friend's head. Accidentally." She mimed quotation marks with her fingers. "Joe had to pick him up from school. Supposedly, Joe's going to make him read, but that man thought it was funny. So who knows how well he'll follow through. And then one of my contracts fell apart. Failed inspection." She sighed and grabbed her menu. "Now, I'm starving." She pulled on her glasses to read. "How was the computer situation?"

"I don't know yet. The guy seemed confident he could figure out what happened. I should hear from Scott anytime. Hopefully sooner than later." I closed my eyes. "I just realized I'm going to have to drive all the way back to Lochsloy to pick it up. Why did Uncle Chris have to find one so far away?"

She squeezed a lemon into her tea. "He said this guy is an expert in Trojan horses and other hacks. Chris has a lot of respect for him. Don't worry. Scott will figure out what is going on."

The waitress returned, and we ordered. I chose the crispy calamari, and Kari picked the lasagna. Anticipating the food, I relaxed back in my seat.

Kari added sugar to her tea. "So, who do you think did it?"

I laughed. If that wasn't the question of the hour. "I have no idea."

She stirred her drink briskly. "Sure you do. You have a knack for this stuff. Did you hear anything that day?"

I thought about it. "Maybe. But I had no idea anything was wrong until Andy came screaming out of the Range Rover."

"With the waves on the lake and being inside the house, it would be hard to hear anything." She frowned. "Hardcastle must have known the murderer, or he would have shouted."

I shivered and took a sip. The sweet/sour rolled over my tongue. "That feels worse to me for some reason. I kind of thought it was just a stranger that someone hired. Maybe a neighbor, even." The theory built up in my mind. I could practically see it happening. "The man walked up to the Range Rover's window, so Hardcastle unrolled his window to answer. And then—!" My dramatic pause alluded to what happened next.

Kari frowned, unimpressed. "Madison Estate, right? Isn't that in the middle of nowhere?"

Just like that, she popped the balloon of my theory. It couldn't have been the neighbor. "Yes, you're right," I answered glumly. Then another thought came to me. "But the lake is right there. Maybe that's how they got in."

"By boat?"

"Yes! Exactly." I leaned forward, excited. "If they had a boat just down the bank, we would have never seen it. He could have killed Hardcastle and escaped by water. I bet that's what happened."

"What about the guy in the woods?" Kari sipped her lemonade.

That woman had a good memory. I blew out a breath. "Maybe he was on his way to the shore when we spotted him. Or he had a buddy. I'm not sure. But, in the end, he made a clean escape."

Kari nodded. "I can see that."

I swirled my ice with my straw. "The thing that doesn't make sense is why the murderer involved me? The whole thing was a setup. The house was never for sale. The email contacting Uncle Chris disappeared."

"Probably eaten by the same program that went after your computer."

"Andy said he was going to rake through Hardcastle's information and track it down."

Right then our food came. I never saw anything that looked so wonderful and realized I was starving. Of course, the food came with several sauces, and soon I was dipping both fries and calamari. It tasted wonderful.

Kari typed on her phone. "So, Hardcastle had several enemies."

I nodded. "He was a realtor mogul, so I believe that."

"And he was after a certain hospital. Have you looked into this?"

I shook my head. "Not yet. But Andy was telling me something about it."

"Check it out," she encouraged. "I read about it in Forbes magazine."

"What hospital?"

"Saint Charity in Philadelphia."

I typed in the name Hardcastle and the name of the hospital into my phone. The story came up, alright. Along with photos filled with protestors.

"You can't tear down a hospital and not expect blowback," Kari said sagely and reached over to snag one of my fries. "Maybe it came back to really bite him big time."

"Do you know if the police were investigating the protestors?"

"I'm assuming so." She went back to her lasagna, scooping up a massive bite with a long string of cheese.

I scanned the news story. A woman with long blonde hair stood out in the background. I've heard of people who rub you the wrong way at first sight, but this might be my first experience. Something about her eyes just set my teeth on edge. They were heavily made up, but that wasn't the problem. A lot of my friends loved the mall's makeup counter. No, this had something to do with a certain hardness that had been captured in the camera flash glint.

"You ever see her before?" I asked, pushing my phone forward.

Kari studied the screen. "Erika Marsh. She's a well-known activist in the area. She's tough."

I clicked the article and read, "Activist takes on biggest real-estate builder in a toe-to-toe battle."

"Huh. Marsh. I remember Andy mentioning the name but for some reason I pictured a man." I read further. "It says Hardcastle's attorney filed to delay the court case."

"He's going to bleed her dry in the courts. That's what happens when you fight with someone who has bags of money to spare. It's hard to win as the underdog."

"So, you might resort to doing anything to win?" I raised an eyebrow before grabbing a calamari ring.

She nodded. "You never know. But check this out as well." Reaching over, she absconded my phone and started typing. After a minute of scrolling, she stabbed something and then pushed the phone back in my direction.

I glanced down. She'd found another news story, one of those sensational news blogs. This one was entirely different. "Mr. Hardcastle is a brand new father."

"What?" I gasped.

"And her father hated him. So the story heats up." She lifted an eyebrow and shoved another bite in her mouth.

CHAPTER TWELVE

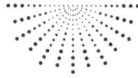

*K*ari and I headed back to the office. To be honest, information spun around in my head like confetti in the wind. I couldn't wait to get back at my desk and do a search for Erika Marsh, the activist. Not to mention Hardcastle's baby momma.

Of course, as soon as I walked into the building, I realized I didn't have a computer anymore.

Kari grabbed her portfolio and left to meet some clients.

I sank in my chair and twirled around, wondering what to do next. Most of my work required a PC. I stared at my phone, willing it to ring with someone wanting a house showing.

Who knew where Uncle Chris was at?

I spun around to stare at his office door. He'd left it cracked open… a tempting crack. A crazy idea came to mind. How mad would he be if I used his computer? He couldn't be too angry, could he?

Deciding I might as well see if I could even log in, I jumped up with my folder of clients and went in.

As usual, his office was a total mess. Might as well do some good if I was going to borrow his PC. I loaded the trash with all the fast-food containers, used napkins, and soda bottles. I carried out the coffee mugs and rinsed them in the sink. I filled one mug with water and took it to his dying plant. After giving it a drink, I moved it closer to the window and angled the blinds so some light would fall on the poor thing. I snagged the carpet sweeper and sucked up what looked like a pile of nacho chips and other crumbs from around his chair. Last but not least, I dampened a paper towel to clean off the coffee rings and other unidentifiable splotches from the desktop.

Feeling like I'd earned the privilege, I scooted the chair closer to the keyboard, hit the power button, and immediately frowned.

It needed a password.

At that point, I gave up and texted Uncle Chris — **Hey, can I use your computer for a bit?**

He texted right back. — **Sure- password is Rusty Rooster.**

I grinned as I typed it in. I should have known he'd use the name of his favorite bar.

I logged into my work page and found the contracts that needed to be signed. Once finished, I immediately dove into what had been in the back of my mind. Using the search engine, I typed in Erika Marsh.

Who was this activist who had taken on Hardcastle, anyway?

The same news shot popped up from before. I scrolled through the list to see other things she'd supported. After a few minutes, I concluded she apparently had political aspirations and wanted to run for congress.

I rubbed my neck. So a win for Erika with saving this hospital would be a big deal for her career. Seemed to be a motive to have it out for Mr. Hardcastle.

My cell phone rang. I flipped it over to see an unknown number.

"Hello. Stella O'Neil," I answered.

"This is Scott about your computer. I found something interesting you might like to know."

"Oh, tell me!" I leaned forward, excited.

"You know how your uncle had me check over his, and I found the hallmark of a known hacker?"

"Yes. A smilie face."

"That's right. Well, I found the same thing on yours."

"Really? Dennis Clark, the hacker from Australia? But why would he even care about me?"

"He's about the biggest gun out there, to be honest. I have no idea. You midnight for US security?" he joked.

"I'm a nobody, seriously. Hardcastle was the biggest client I've ever had. And it seems like there would be easier ways to shut someone's computer down."

"Oh, he wasn't trying to shut it down," he responded.

"What? Why did he do it, then?"

"Mirroring. He downloaded all your information to a remote site. Every keystroke, every email you've ever made. He's looking for something. You have any idea what that could be?"

My tongue dried up like a slice of bread left out in the sun. I couldn't believe the violation of privacy. And when I thought of my personal emails, ones to Dad where we were fighting, ones looking for information about Mom, ones to Carlson... my face flamed with heat.

I cleared my throat. "I'm not sure. I'm pretty boring."

"Well, I have the report downloaded, and I already put a call into the number of the detective your Uncle said was working on the case. I just thought you'd like to know."

"Okay," I mumbled. "Can I get my computer now?"

"It's trash. You'll never be able to use it again. Besides, I'm pretty sure the cops will want it as evidence. In the future, be very careful opening up any email attachments. Hackers know how to manipulate you to make you feel the email is urgent. Don't fall for it."

"Hackers," I snorted angrily.

"Yeah, especially ones like Dennis. To be honest, I feel honored to work on a machine he messed with." He swallowed and then added, "Sorry about that."

"No worries. When I screw up, I only do it with the best."

"At least you're a good sport about it."

We hung up, and I sat there numbly. Why would a criminal of that caliber want to come after me? How did he even know who I was?

Second question, and probably more important, what was he hoping to find? My grocery list? Complaining emails? My clients' names?

I texted Uncle Chris. —**Bad news. My computer is toast and most likely will be held for evidence. Is there any way you can get me a new one?**

I waited to see if he'd answer. It showed read and then nothing. Great.

Finally, he texted back. — **I'll look into it. In the meantime, use mine.**

I realized then the hacker had all my information. Including my bank information, my social security number, and my credit cards. Groaning, I dialed the number for the bank to have them issue me new cards. Then I looked into a credit check to have someone protect me against identity fraud.

It was expensive. I texted Uncle Chris again. — **I don't suppose insurance will cover me paying for identity fraud coverage?**

He wrote back. — **Good idea. Just do it. I'll cover you.**

Sighing, I stared back at the computer screen where Erika's smug face smiled at me. Somehow I felt entangled with her through this whole debacle.

"Did you do it?" I asked her. "Did you hire someone to kill him?"

"Did she kill who?" a voice asked.

CHAPTER THIRTEEN

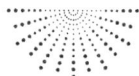

*M*y heart leaped nearly into my throat, and I stared wildly at the doorway. Kari stood there, her eyebrows lifted to high heavens at my reaction.

"Sorry," I said, trying to catch my breath.

"Wow, you must have been really focused not to have heard me come in. Here, I got you this." She tossed a magazine on the desk. The main headline screamed, "Bigfoot seen by the White House."

"Huh?" I could feel my eyebrows twist in confusion.

She glanced to see what had me so perplexed. "Not that one. Read the one below."

In a smaller box, a headline asked the question, "Will a two-month-old ruin the real estate mogul's empire?"

I nodded. "Wow, quite the headline."

"That's Hardcastle's baby's mother. Her name is Margaret Brooke. Look her up."

I turned to the keyboard and typed. Moments later, a woman, appearing in her mid-twenties, gorgeous in every way, showed up in images. A random headline showed up asking, "Trouble in Paradise?"

"Marriage issues?" I muttered, and clicked through a link.

"They always say that about celebrity marriages." Kari came around back to read over my shoulder. The photos showed the journey of an aspiring young model to the now wife of a very powerful man, Hardcastle.

One photo caught my attention. In it, Margaret's face appeared decidedly less beautifully posed.

Kari snorted. "It cracks me up to see people angry when they've had that much botox."

I clicked the article attached to the angry picture and quickly scanned through to the bottom.

Kari ignored me, still affected by Margaret's expression. "I mean, the poor thing hasn't even had a chance to perfect her adult femme de fatale. It should be illegal to have all that plastic surgery, especially at that age. Why would she do that to herself?"

"Some women feel pressured," I mumbled, trying to concentrate on the reading material. "Especially models."

"Yeah, well, she looks more surprised than angry."

"She's angry, all right." I pointed to the screen. "Read right there. She's going after that activist, Erika Marsh, for attempting to block the sale of Saint Charity hospital. She says that Erika is stopping a progressive move that would give the hospital the funds to move to a newer building with more updated equipment."

"So, now you're saying Saint Charity is the loser?"

"That's Margaret's defense."

"Wild. I can't keep these stories straight."

"My dad used to say there are three sides. Yours, mine, and the truth."

Kari laughed. "I wonder where your dad learned that, because Chris has been saying the same thing for years."

"Oscar." We both grinned.

"What's going on with the hospital now?" Kari asked. "And how strange Erika and Margaret are somewhat connected, if only in a feud."

Good question. I typed in the name. Saint Charity's webpage came up like everything was normal, including driving directions and department phone numbers. I searched to see if there were any recent new stories about the hospital. One popped up with an advertisement to a fundraiser. Apparently they needed ten million dollars to do all the renovations they needed.

The fundraiser article read like a scare tactic. It stated in no uncertain terms that they would lose their federal funding if they didn't do the upgrades to comply with the new laws. I read it out loud to Kari.

When I finished, we stared at each other for a second.

"So maybe it would be beneficial to the hospital if Mr. Hardcastle is allowed to buy it," Kari concluded.

"Makes you wonder which side Erika is really on," I added.

"Maybe there's only one side all along. Hers."

CHAPTER FOURTEEN

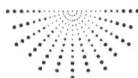

*A*fter tidying up my contracts and following up with my other clients, I felt I'd redeemed the day after the crazy start. I logged out of Uncle Chris's computer and grabbed my stuff. I was ready to go home and collapse on the couch.

Out in the office, Kari packed up her things at her desk.

"Long day, huh?" I said. We walked out of the office together.

She reacted with a big eye roll. "I tell you what, Joe better have had Colby do his homework. And I plan on serving eggs for dinner."

I laughed as we walked to our cars.

When I pulled into my driveway, I spotted Gato, the neighbor's cat, in a predatory position down by a huge lilac bush. I happened to know there was a bird's nest in the upper branches and leaped out of the car as soon as I had it in park.

"Gato!" I called, clapping my hands.

The cat rose to his feet with an annoyed flick of his ear and a swish of his tail.

"What are you doing over there?" I hurried across the lawn and bent to pet the cat. He nudged his cheek in forgiveness against my hand. "I know it's hard and only natural, but you need to leave those birdies alone."

He stalked off in the direction of the neighbors. I still hadn't met them yet. In fact, Gato was just the pet name I called him.

It made me sad now to think that I might never get a chance to know the cat's real name. Not with Mrs. Carmichael selling the home.

Speaking of house sales, a question nagged at me ever since I'd read the article about the hospital. Probably it seemed apparent to anyone else. But I processed things slowly, so it wasn't until now that it came to the forefront of the gray matter.

I walked up the porch steps and dialed Uncle Chris.

"Yello!" he answered.

"Hey, I have a real estate question for you."

Mom waved at me from the kitchen. I waved back and headed for my bedroom.

"Go for it," he said.

"Today, I happened across a story that pertained to a deal that Hardcastle had been trying to put together. It's in court, but the original deal fell through due to public outcry because of a protest."

"Saint Charity Hospital. Sure. I know all about it."

"Well, it looks like the hospital is really struggling. They actually might go under."

"Yeah?" He sounded surprised.

"Right now, they're running a fundraiser to do the upgrades they need to meet the new legal regulations. My question is, what happens if they fail?"

"You mean, if they don't make the money?"

"Yeah. And can't make the changes. What happens to the hospital if they lose the government funding?"

"Well, then the hospital will go into default. They'll have to sell everything off, and the building will go into foreclosure."

"So, it will still be sold," I confirmed.

"Yeah, but at a much lower price than what Hardcastle offered. It could end up in a bidding war, but even in that case, the price will only rise up to about half what the property is worth. It's what makes foreclosures so popular."

"Interesting." I sat on my bed. "Thank you."

"You get that identity thing sorted out?"

"Yeah. I signed up. What a pain. Thanks for paying for it."

"Hey, it's not everyone who attracts the attention of a hacker like Dennis Clark. I feel like we've been touched by royalty or something."

"Or something." I scowled. "I'm the one who had all of her private stuff sifted through."

"This is a weird one, that's for sure. But we'll get it sorted out soon."

With that, he said goodbye and hung up. There was a tap on my door.

"Come in!" I yelled.

Mom peeked in. "Hi, honey. I wanted to bring you some cookies."

I patted the bed next to me. It was still so odd not to be alone in the house. Not to mention having her here doing the things for me she would have done when I was a kid.

She walked in with a plate emanating the most wonderful chocolate gooey vanilla scent. "I'm having fun in the kitchen," she said, shrugging a shoulder almost apologetically. "It's a lot easier than making food in the big house."

"You made food?"

"Oh, yeah." She sat down next to me, and her thin frame scarcely made the bed jiggle. "I was known as the birthday cake queen. I made them for all the girls. So, what are you working on now?" she asked. "Am I interrupting? You were on the phone a moment ago."

"No, you're not interrupting. I am still kind of poking around Mr. Hardcastle's death."

"I'm sure the police are doing their best."

"Yeah, I know. But it feels so personal since it happened while I was there. Like only a few steps away." My fingers trailed up to my throat. "I can't explain why, but it feels like it's somehow my fault."

"Your fault?" Mom's eyebrows rose. "Why would you think that?"

"I don't know. Like I should have heard something or seen someone and been able to stop it. I just can't believe it happened while I was wandering through a house, completely oblivious."

Mom patted my knee. "You know you're not to blame. But I hear what you're saying. I get it. But the reality is we can't control other people's choices. That person knew you were in there and did it anyway. They were very determined. Maybe if you'd come out of the house sooner, you would have been killed as well." Mom took a sudden breath. "Stella, I couldn't have handled that. Found you again only to lose you." Her voice trailed away until the last word was a whisper.

"Aww." I gave her a big hug. "I couldn't have either."

"Well, you'd be dead," she pointed out pragmatically.

I laughed. "I mean, I couldn't bear to lose you either."

She hugged me back. It was strange how little she was in my big grown-up arms. But I still kind of fit. I wiggled until my head was on her shoulder, and she patted my back the way I remembered when I was six. Hot tears unexpectedly sprang into my eyes. We stayed that way for a moment, with her patting and me relaxing.

Finally, I sat up. "I love you, Mom."

"I love you too, chickee." She held her hand out then, palm toward me. I placed my hand over hers and smiled as we both relived the game we'd played years ago.

"Now, back to Hardcastle's death. What do you have so far?" Her face reverted to all business. She grabbed a cookie and nibbled as she waited for me to answer.

I took a cookie as well and filled her in on what I'd learned so far. "Mostly, I've been looking into this hospital deal. It was the last big one Hardcastle was involved in before coming out to look at the Madison Estate. Though it was taken to court, the deal completely fell apart due to public pressure. And from what I've learned, it seems like an activist named Erika Marsh was the ringleader behind that."

"And who's Erika Marsh?"

I nodded. "Good question."

My thumbs flew over the keyboard as I entered her name again. I saw her newest cause seemed to have been organizing a protest to the tearing out of apartment buildings to put in a business center.

Interestingly enough, right in the middle of all these articles, I spotted a red carpet photo. I clicked on it, and it brought me to one of those gossip sites. The title simply stated that Erika was a guest at the event. There was also a series of pictures, so I clicked through them.

My eyebrows raised. The third one in starred Tristen Smith, the realtor guru with the golden car. Something had to be up here. I could feel it. I searched the event for more information, but it was just more pseudo-celebrity pictures.

I closed the page and went back to the search engine. On a hunch, I typed in both Tristen Smith and Erika Marsh to see if anything would come up.

Something surely did. A photo saying the two had left the event together that night.

Sounded awful chummy-like. My spidey sense tingled.

CHAPTER FIFTEEN

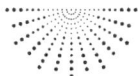

I pointed to the picture of Tristen Smith. "That's Hardcastle's competitor! Or was."

Mom understood the implications right away. "Wow."

"I've got to call Carlson," I said, jumping up and nearly knocking over the plate of cookies.

Mom nodded and headed out. I discovered that was one amazing thing about her. She knew how to give space, and she was not easily offended.

I wanted to be more like her.

But for now, I texted Carlson—**please call me!**

* * *

UNFORTUNATELY, it was several hours before I heard from him other than frantic text messaging. Dinner time swelled and passed. Mom and I played checkers in front of Jeopardy. The moon rose, and Mom went to bed. I soon followed.

Then the phone rang.

"Carlson!" I shouted after snatching it up.

"Hello, yourself," he answered. "Sorry it took so long, but tonight's been crazy."

Of course, I understood. I quickly filled him in.

There was a lengthy pause after I finished. "Carlson?" I asked, making sure we hadn't been disconnected.

"I hear what you're saying," Carlson said slowly. "But there's a few things in this theory of yours that aren't adding up."

"What's not adding up?" I demanded. "Erika Marsh was with Tristan, the real estate tycoon, and Hardcastle's rival. Later, the hacker that went after my computer was seen in town. It makes perfect sense."

"We need to figure out a motive then, other than competition or your spidey sense. It'll never fly with my chief if I say my girlfriend has a hunch."

I could feel myself ruffle. "Of course you can. Because it all makes sense."

"It's a theory, that's true. And you found a couple of interesting photographs online. But we need evidence to support this."

Carlson always questioned everything. My itty bitty inner voice reminded me that's what made him a good cop. However, right now, I wanted his excitement.

I shot a new theory at him. "I think I know how he got away."

"He, who?"

The man was trying to irritate me, I swear. "The murderer, of course."

"Alright. Let's hear it."

"The lake! I bet he arrived by water." I smiled, proudly.

Again this was met by silence. After a few seconds, he answered thoughtfully, "Okay, I can see that. What say we go see for ourselves and see if there are boat tracks."

"Really? I'd love that!"

"I'm off tomorrow. Let me give the detective a call to make sure it's okay with him. Don't want to step on any toes."

* * *

THE NEXT AFTERNOON, after receiving the okay, he swung by my house to pick me up. We had the windows rolled down, and the fresh air ruffled my hair into crazy waves. Music blasted from the radio, and I tipped my head back to smile.

"What are you grinning at?" Carlson asked. Coincidentally, he was grinning as well.

"I'm just so happy. I love these kinds of days."

I think he liked that answer, because his smile grew. His hand rested lazily on the steering wheel. His other snuck over and grabbed mine. My heart tingled to see our fingers entwined. I could do this all day.

Soon we were closing in on Madison Estate, up into the mountain and past all the fancy mansions, and now headed down the other side. After a moment, I untangled our hands and looked up Erika again.

For being an advocate, her public profile remained surprisingly elusive. She seemed to be embroiled in her new battle against an apartment building in New York. I did manage to track down a phone number and a place of employment.

"What are you doing?" Carlson asked.

"Checking out that activist that went up against Hardcastle. You did tell me to find a better motive. Did you know she works in New York City?"

"Where at?"

"Barrington Towers."

"Those are new," Carlson said. "I know because I have a buddy that left the force and was hired by them for security. He gets paid top dollar."

"Oh, you jealous?" I smiled.

"I'd never work there. Tristen owns them."

"Wait, what? Tristen Smith? So maybe there's something to that photograph of them leaving the gala together. You think they're dating?"

"I don't know. Anything is possible."

"Well, that sure makes them even more suspect. I bet both of their fingerprints are all over Mr. Hardcastle's death."

"Motives, Stella. We need to find motives."

He pulled down the driveway to the empty house. I couldn't help the shiver that ran down my spine as I stared at the house's empty windows.

Carlson's gaze flickered over to me. "You going to be okay?"

"I hadn't realized how seeing it again would affect me. This is so weird. His Range Rover was right there." I pointed ahead.

"Right in the middle of the driveway, huh?"

I nodded.

"And where were you?"

"I parked behind him. Right about where we are now."

Carlson pulled the e-brake and stared at the forest through the windshield. The water lapped the shore with soft waves. I could hear it even from here.

"Where did you see the gunman?"

I pointed to the woods on the side of us. "Right over there. Andy saw him and ran out."

"He ran toward the gunman?"

"Wait. No." I rubbed my temples, trying to remember. "Andy was over there earlier. When we saw the gunman, we were both in the car. I stepped on the gas and backed out as fast as I could."

"And there were no other cars around?"

I shook my head in the negative. "They must have come by the water. There's a dock over there."

Carlson glanced in that direction. His hand tightened on my leg in a supportive way. "You feel comfortable to get out?"

I nodded.

We climbed from the car and met in front of the hood.

"I also received permission from the owners for us to be here. We're just going to take a quick peek around since I'm not actually on the case. Come on. Let's go check out the dock."

He took a few steps in that direction. Reluctantly, I hung behind. I stared at the woods, suddenly very afraid. Anyone could be out there right now. Anyone might be watching.

Carlson noticed my hesitance. He glanced at the woods and then back at me. "It's okay. We're safe." He reached for my hand, and I gave it to him.

"Wow, you're freezing." He rubbed my palm between his two warm and overly-large ones, and we walked down to the dock.

It was a floating dock with a covered boat-lift at the end. As we stepped out onto it, Carlson released my hand and strode to the end of the dock. The slight unstable bobbing surprised me for a moment as I caught my balance.

He turned around. "You can see the car from here?"

I looked and saw the vehicle. "Yep."

He squatted down by the depth pole. The water splashing against it was murky with floating bits of who knew what.

Slowly, he rose to his feet and made his way back toward me. Taking my hand again, we left the lift and walked along the shore.

It was rocky here, with round stones and boulders and ancient monstrous trees that a windstorm had carried across the lake. Their bark had long disappeared, and the trees lay like gray dinosaur bones stacked on shore.

"Ready to head back to the car?" he asked.

"Can't find anything?"

He shook his head. "The shore is too stony. I'm not seeing anything. You?"

I loved that he included me. "Nope."

We walked back to the house, where he circled it once and then stood on the deck. Cupping his eyes, he peered into the windows.

"We spent most of our time in the kitchen," I said.

"On the opposite side of the driveway."

I nodded. "Maybe that's why I didn't hear anything."

He came over and hugged me. "It would be hard to hear anything inside the house and over the waves. There's nothing you could have done. It's not your fault."

I sank against him. That hot, horrid guilt was still a companion, but I appreciated his support. "I feel like it is."

"I promise it's not. It's the person who wielded the knife, no matter what. Now, come on."

"Where we going?"

"I have one more thing to look at."

"What's that?"

"I want to go over the property. Where exactly was the gunman located?"

CHAPTER SIXTEEN

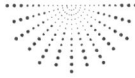

I stopped Carlson. "Before we go, just give me a second. I need to make a quick phone call."

Scrolling back through my earlier search results, I found the link to Barrington Towers and dialed.

A woman answered, sounding young and peppy. "Towers Incorporated, How can I direct your call?"

"Hi there," I said. I smiled to sound friendly and hoped she could hear it. "Is there an Erika Marsh who works there?"

Her voice sharpened. "What is it you're inquiring about?

I smiled harder. "I was curious if she might be connected with a real estate deal I'm checking into out here."

"I'll give her your message." The phone disconnected.

I frowned. I hadn't left a message, so how could she pass one on?

"You ready?" Carlson asked.

I nodded and tucked the phone away, feeling very dissatisfied.

"So, after you discovered Mr. Hardcastle, the two of you went back to your car?"

I gestured to where I'd been parked. "I went alone. Andy was pretty upset and wandered around for a minute to try and to calm down."

"And then what happened?"

"I realized the murderer could still be in the area, so I called to Andy. He hurried over, and we both got into my car." I shook my head. "The poor guy was a wreck."

"And then?"

What, was this an interrogation? I'd told Carlson all this before. "Well, I called the police and reported what happened. The rest is kind of a blur."

"Try hard to remember. What happened next?"

"Someone showed up in the woods with a rifle." I winced at the memory. "It was one of the most frightening things to ever happen to me. I felt trapped. I didn't know how many people were hiding out there. It was terrifying." I felt my anxiety rising now as I stared at the woods.

"Aw, honey." He rubbed my arm. "I'm sorry. Did you see what he was wearing?"

I thought about it. "I saw the rifle. The guy was hidden in the trees."

"Where was he at? What direction?" Carlson scanned the trees.

"Over there."

"You mind if I go look? Want to come?"

I hesitated for a second. Did I really want to do that? My entire stomach flopped over. What would Dad tell me? Actually, Dad would probably say duck for cover. But what about Oscar? My grandfather would tell me to get back on that horse. I couldn't let the memory beat me.

Carlson waited patiently, and I immediately felt encouraged by the kindness in his eyes. He didn't say anything. He also wasn't going to give me the easy way out and tell me to wait in the car. He watched me like he knew I could do it.

I knew I could, too. I nodded and reached for his hand. He grabbed it, his hand warm and strong, and we crossed the driveway and moved into the trees.

The dense forest immediately closed in around us. I took a deep breath and tried to steady myself from this weird feeling of being smothered.

"We're safe. I promise," Carlson said.

I wasn't so sure.

About twenty feet from the driveway, I stopped. "Right here is where we saw him."

Carlson nodded, his gaze sweeping the area. "You mind if we go in a little bit farther?"

I nodded, resigned. Not ten feet from where we stood, Carlson pointed. "Look at that. What does it remind you of?"

I focused on the tree he meant. It had been dead for years and stripped of bark. One thin branch stood straight out.

"What do you think? Could that look like a rifle from the road?"

"Maybe." I felt confused. The more I looked, the more it seemed Carlson could be right. Had the whole thing just been our imaginations, fueled by panic and shock? "This is so disappointing."

"Disappointing how?" He bent down to study the ground. Apparently, it was nothing because he stood again.

"That I could be tricked like that. I'm frustrated I didn't keep a clear head."

"You were exposed to very stressful circumstances. Someone had just been murdered. I'm impressed with how well you did. Give yourself some credit."

I sighed. There was nothing I could do to change things now.

We walked back out to the driveway.

At the car, Carlson turned and looked over the trees again.

My phone rang with a call from Uncle Chris. "Hello," I said.

"Stella, what have you done?"

I straightened like I was in trouble. "What do you mean?"

"I just had a call here, threatening to slap you and Flamingo Realty with a cease-and-desist."

"Huh?" I gasped, completely flummoxed.

"Yeah, by a snooty lawyer representing a woman named Erika Marsh."

My jaw dropped. "Carlson!" I called.

He turned around at the panic in my voice. "What's the matter?"

"Remember how I called Barrington Towers? Erika's attorney just called Uncle Chris."

He whistled. "Wow, went straight to your employer. Trying to get you fired, maybe."

Uncle Chris chuckled. "Too bad they don't realize we are blood. You take one of us on, you take us all."

"I don't get it, Uncle Chris. The secretary or whoever she was hung up before I gave any personal information. How did she know it was me who called?"

"I have no idea."

I rubbed my neck, where my muscles throbbed from stress. "You think it has to do with my computer being hacked? Can they trace my phone?"

He groaned. "Let me call my friend who's a detective. He's the one checking into the two computer jobs."

"What? It's a case now?"

"Yea. They consider it a hostile takeover of some very sensitive information. The fact that he stole information on a business computer is a big deal. Much bigger than if this was your personal computer."

"Okay. Ask him right away. I need to know if I should get a new phone or something."

"I will. You guys find anything out at the estate?"

My cheeks burned, and I couldn't admit I'd mistaken a tree branch for a rifle. "Not really," I hedged.

"Well, take care of yourself. I'll let you know if I hear anything new."

"Got it. See you soon."

I hung up and stared at Carlson. "Can you believe they called my work?"

"These are the big dogs now," he said and jumped into the driver's seat. I stared out into the forest before getting in. That stupid branch seemed to mock me as he backed out of the driveway.

I tried to encourage myself as we turned onto the road. Silly phrases like, "I didn't know. I did the best I could. Other people might have freaked out the same way."

None of them helped.

My phone rang.

"Miss O'Neil?" a smooth male voice asked.

I felt instantly on guard. "Yes?"

"How was your little drive up to the estate today, young lady?"

Every hair on my neck stood up. I could scarcely breathe. "Who is this?" I finally asked.

"Who is it?" Carlson demanded, noticing the immediate change in me.

The man continued smoothly. "Don't worry about me. I know a lot about you. More than you could even realize. I think it's time you start to mind your own business. There's a lot of it, I see. Tell your mother hello from us. She's quite the gardener."

I didn't answer.

"Who is it?" Carlson demanded again. "Give me the phone."

I handed it over.

"Officer Carlson here. Who are you? Hello?" He stared at the phone. "He hung up. What did he say?"

I repeated the conversation. "I wish I'd put it on speaker. I was too shocked."

Carlson swore and hit the steering wheel. Then he grabbed his phone from his front pocket. A moment later, he had the detective to the murder case on the line.

"Your witness is being threatened," he said. He went on to talk about my computer being hacked and the threat of a cease-and-desist. "I think she needs some eyes on her home."

CHAPTER SEVENTEEN

*C*arlson squeezed the steering wheel as the muscles in his jaw strained in a tight grimace. "I don't like that, not at all."

"Somehow they knew it was me. They must be tracking my number." I stared at my phone like it was the enemy. "Could they be tracing the phone?"

"You mean with the Find My Phone app?"

I nodded.

His nostrils flared. "Let's go get you a new one."

I covered my face. I needed this number. It's how my clients knew to find me. *Breathe, Stella.* "I think I need to go chill out or something."

"You okay?" His eyebrows lifted.

"Nope. Not at all. To be honest, I didn't realize how much this would affect me."

"Where do you want to go?" He asked.

I glanced at him. "What about Oscar's house?"

"You think he'll be okay with us dropping in?"

"Of course," I said.

"I mean, me. You think he'll be okay with me stopping by?"

Actually, that was a great question. I lifted my finger to indicate I needed a second and dialed Oscar's number. I couldn't help but feel sick, thinking this call might be logged in by someone I didn't want to know.

My grandfather answered with his usual charming aplomb. "You better not be a car warranty caller."

"Oscar, it's me."

"Oh," His voice rose into something considerably more cheerful. "Stella. What are you up to?"

"Do you mind if we stop by for a minute?"

"Sure." And there was the pause I'd expected. He asked suspiciously, "Who's we?"

"Carlson and me."

"Hmm, I guess you'll want me to put the kettle on, then. Probably have to find matching mugs."

"Don't worry about that. Want me to bring anything?"

"What? You need more than tea?"

"Yeah. I'm hungry."

"Let's see how this guy does around the kitchen with grilled cheese."

I bit back a smile and said goodbye.

"What did he say?" Carlson asked.

"I think he might be giving you a test."

"A test, huh?"

"He wants to know if you can make a grilled cheese."

Carson laughed. "Of course I can. How else do you think I've kept myself fed all these years? That, and mountains of scrambled eggs, with the occasional refried bean sandwich."

I made a face. "You're not serious?'

"Yeah, I know how to make grilled cheese."

"No, I mean that you've eaten the bean sandwich."

"Don't knock it until you've tried it." He grinned, proud of himself that he managed to gross me out.

I shook my head. "Thanks all the same." The very thought made my stomach turn.

We pulled down the driveway. I smiled to see Oscar waiting for us on the porch with Peanut in his arms. He didn't look at me though, instead stared at Carlson, his eyebrows lowered and forehead rumpled.

"Oh, boy," Carlson muttered as he shifted the car into park. "You weren't kidding about that test."

"It'll be fine," I lied. I hurried up the stairs and hugged Oscar. Peanut tried her best to give me kisses, so I didn't give much of a verbal greeting.

He patted my back and then resumed his scowl at Carlson. His expression reminded me of his long FBI career, and I felt impressed.

Carlson sauntered up the stairs. He'd met my grandfather before, but not under the official title of being my boyfriend.

"Sir," he said, dipping his head.

Oscar glared up at him, like a chihuahua at a St. Bernard. If I were a betting woman, I'd put my money on the chihuahua biting first.

"So you guys drove to the estate, huh?" Oscar asked and abruptly spun on a slippered heel back into the house.

Carlson glanced at me, and I shrugged. We followed him inside. I peeked into the kitchen to see that Oscar had put out the teapot and sugar but had left the bread, cheese, and butter in the pantry. He wasn't making it easy on Carlson, that's for sure.

"So, I heard you can make grilled sandwiches. Go on, help yourself," Oscar gruffly told Carlson.

I stood up, ready to rescue him, but Carlson waved me back. "Absolutely. How do you like yours, sir?"

Oscar's eyebrows flicked up. "Slightly golden. Just a little crunch."

Carlson stood in front of the fridge. "Do you mind if I—"

My grandfather shook his head. "No, no. Help yourself."

Carlson opened the fridge and studied the interior. After a second, he pulled out the butter and block of cheese. He found the bread in the bread box, retrieved a pan from one cupboard, and soon was buttering the bread and slicing the cheese.

"So, how important is a cease-and-desist?" I asked Carlson by way of informing Oscar.

"What's this?" Oscar asked. He filled the cups with water from a pot on the stove and set some tea bags in to steep.

I filled Oscar in on the phone call to Barrington Towers and the resulting calls from both the lawyer and the one to my personal phone number.

"What are you doing about all this?" Oscar demanded of Carlson.

"I'm trying to get some protection for her. I don't like it, not at all." He turned the pan on and started to assemble the bread and cheese.

Slightly mollified, Oscar shifted back in my direction. "Any reason why you're setting off these big guns?"

I shook my head. "Other than the fact that they don't like me poking into Erika's background. She's trying to run for congress, and she's fighting to save an apartment building now."

"But Hardcastle didn't buy the hospital after all the backlash she manufactured. So she won, right?"

I shrugged. "There's still a court case going on."

"Even the hospital is scrambling with charity events to make the repairs. Face it, she won. I don't see the court case as a motive for her to murder Mr. Hardcastle. Especially since she's moved on to other causes."

"And one of those goals happens to be in the public eye," Oscar said. He pointed to the morning newspaper which showed Erika's smiling political ad. "Trust me. Right about now, she's trying to watch her P's and Q's because everyone against her will be digging for dirt."

Thus ended my motive for Erika. Back to square one. I couldn't believe it. I thought about Hardcastle's new baby. "I found out Hardcastle just had a son. Did you know that?"

Carlson shook his head. Carefully, he eased a spatula under one of the sandwiches and peeked at the coloring. He set it down and pressed the top of the bread.

I pulled the tea bag from the mug and set it on a paper towel. "His name is Marcus."

"Being born is not much of a motive, Hollywood. I think you can rule Marcus out," Carlson teased.

"You're a dork. Anyway, there were rumors that the baby's mom, Margaret, and Hardcastle were headed for divorce."

Carlson flipped the grilled cheese. Oscar pushed his glasses further up his nose and watched. I thought the fact that Oscar didn't comment was a sign of approval.

"So, did they get divorced or not?"

"I'm trying to find out." I frowned and typed into my phone. I shook my head. "I can't tell. No one's reporting it."

The Pomeranian danced at Carlson's feet.

"Surprised they're doing this so soon after the baby," Oscar said. He whistled for the dog. "Come here, Bear."

She jumped up and raked those sharp claws down Carlson's shin, and I saw him wince.

"Bear!" Oscar scolded. "You come here right now, you fluffy food bucket."

The dog sassily stared back, tongue hanging up, with nary a move.

"Peanut," I called.

The dog flew to me like she'd suddenly sprouted wings. With one nimble leap, she landed in my lap. Before I could react, her front paws were on the table to examine any goodies that might be within reach.

Oscar scowled and looked away.

"So, what's the law then, if they divorced. Who inherits Hardcastle's estate?" I thought about the divorce proceedings. "Do you think Hardcastle changed his will?"

"I don't know, but I think we can find out. His stuff is in probate right now."

"I can answer this one," Oscar said. "This state has a fifty/fifty split between wife and children. And if there is no wife, the kid gets everything."

"Everything?" I swallowed, thinking about the vast real estate empire.

He nodded.

"So if there is a divorce, then little Marcus is the sole heir."

"Yeah."

Carlson placed a plate of grilled cheese in front of me. The cheese oozed out, and the bread was a lovely crispy golden brown. Peanut was instantly interested, freezing with just her little nose quivering.

Of course, I had to give the pup a corner. She took it gently like a little lady.

"But either way, Margaret benefits because she is the child's caretaker."

"True, unless the child isn't his. Then she gets nothing," Carlson said.

"Her whole life would be different. Most people in that situation couldn't live with that."

"They'd do anything to keep it from happening," Oscar said emphatically. "Good food, Carlson. Next time, let's see how you do with steak."

"Steak, sir?"

"Sounds like a plan. You bring it."

Carlson glanced at me, and I shrugged. No one could outsmart Oscar, that's for sure. He always was one step ahead.

CHAPTER EIGHTEEN

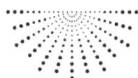

*C*asual conversation peppered the rest of our mealtime. By "casual," I meant that Carlson tried to start small talk, Oscar ignored him and ate, and I lobbed easy questions back to keep the conversation going. Eventually, we all gave up. Afterward, I gathered the dishes and brought them to the sink while Carlson played with his phone. I saw he was texting.

My movement seemed to loosen Oscar's tongue. "So, what's your uncle doing to keep you safe?"

"He hired an identity protection firm since my computer was searched," I answered.

"He better do more," Oscar grumbled.

"I think you need a new phone—a temporary one," Carlson said to respond to my expression of alarm. "No one will be able to track you. You can use your old one once they get caught."

The thought made me both sad and worried. Oscar stooped to give his last piece of crust to Peanut and then drained his tea. Carlson's phone dinged. He studied it with a frown and then typed with his funny index finger pokes.

I ran the water and squirted some soap on the sponge, then set to washing the dishes. As I worked, Oscar put away the cheese and bread.

Suddenly, Carlson rose to his feet. "Hey—" He looked very distracted. "I need to get going. You have some time to come with me?"

"Uh, yeah." I finished the last dish and put it in the rack. "What's up?"

"I think I found an *in* to a few questions we've had."

"Really? You mean we might finally get some answers?"

He nodded. Excited, I dried my hands and stooped to give Peanut some goodbye cuddles. Carlson thanked Oscar for his hospitality. They shook hands, which made me very happy, and then we left for his car.

I climbed in and snapped the seatbelt. "Where we going?"

He grinned like he was about to hand me a surprise birthday cake. "Hardcastle's house."

I made an unintentional ugly sound. "You're kidding me."

He shook his head. "Would I kid you, Hollywood? My good buddy Shepherd is there. We went to the academy together years ago. He works as security at the estate while his wife is the chef. Let's have a chat with him, maybe a beer. See what he says."

I sank back into the seat with a big smile. Somehow, this guy always came through for me.

It was a good while later before we finally drove through a fancy neighborhood. This one had a gated entrance. Carlson pulled up to the key box and punched in the code.

I raised an eyebrow at him, and he shrugged. "Shepherd gave it to me," he explained as we pulled into the ritzy neighborhood.

Talk about out of my pay grade. These houses were places I'd only seen on TV in shows depicting millionaires. Each one had to be worth upwards of twenty million, with lawns greener than anything from a cartoon.

Carlson turned down a perfectly manicured driveway to a monstrosity at the end. Shiny black pillars, red sandstone, and more, the building was as large as a department store. Waiting at the end was a man about the size of a tank with a crew cut and dressed in khakis. He waved, just a single motion, and pointed to where Carlson could park, using hand signals like he was directing an airplane.

"Let me guess. Shepherd?" I asked.

"You got it." Carlson pulled in behind the eight-car separate garage and climbed out of the car. I followed. Shepherd strode over and offered Carlson his hand. His arm looked bigger than my leg.

They shook, and then Shepherd studied me with sparkling green eyes. He smiled. "Come on inside." He waved us in.

The rich green of the lawn took my breath away. I'd never seen grass that shade of emerald before. At the center stood a white bubbling fountain, which had rainbow sprays of water glistening in the sunlight.

Of course, I wondered what would happen to the property. Would Margaret be forced to sell it?

In the exact second, I felt ashamed that I'd be thinking these things. The poor guy wasn't even buried yet.

We headed inside the mansion. The interior blew me away, and that was saying something. I'd seen a lot of homes.

Shepherd led us down a long hallway decorated with family paintings of Hardcastle and his wife on the wall. My steps slowed until I stopped before one. This was the first time I actually had a look at the man so close up and with so much detail.

His expression most likely meant to be stoic and respectable, but somehow, it came across as if he had just sucked on a lemon wedge. Slightly puckered lips, pained squint to the eyes. Speaking of eyes, they were a dark brown, framed by a thick set of eyelashes and near-black eyebrows. His hair swooped to the side in an impressive wave.

Shepherd led us into a small sitting room. A moment later, a woman showed up and was introduced as his wife, Amy.

"So, I'm guessing Mrs. Hardcastle doesn't live here," I said.

"Nope. She has her own place ever since they filed for separation," Shepherd answered, and sat in an armchair.

"Are they officially divorced then?" I asked, taking a seat across from him on the couch.

He nodded. "Hardcastle pushed it through."

"So, who does this house belong to now?" I asked.

"Once probate finishes, baby Marcus will own everything."

"Does he have other kids?" Carlson accepted a soda from Amy. She passed one to me as well.

"Just the boy." Here, Shepherd arched an eyebrow mysteriously.

"Nothing can stop that, then? No one can contest it?"

"Not legally," Shepherd said.

"Well," interrupted Amy. "There is one thing that could stop it."

"And what's that?" Carlson asked. He looked to set the soda down on the coffee table, studied the gorgeous wood surface, and opted to hold it instead.

"If someone demands some sort of proof," Amy answered.

"Proof?"

"Yeah, like a paternity suit."

My eyebrows lifted.

"You asked earlier if I knew what caused their separation. I've heard rumors while cooking in the kitchen," Amy said.

"He suspected his son wasn't his?" I clarified.

"You see any pictures of the baby here?" She lifted a sarcastic eyebrow.

That was very true. All those photos and not one with the new baby.

"Is Margaret with anyone new?" I crossed my legs and rested my hands on my knee.

"As of yet, no. At least, not that we know of. We really liked her, so their separation kind of upset the entire staff," Amy answered.

"What about Mr. Hardcastle? Was he known to have other flings?"

Shepherd answered that question. "Any man in that income bracket has rumors floating around. Were they true? Who knows." He shrugged, but his wife added, "I'm sure he did."

I uncrossed my legs and leaned forward. "So there could be men out there who hated him?"

"Definitely." Amy nodded. "But for more reasons than that. This is a cut-throat business. He constantly out-bid people to make money."

"Still, no one you know who hated him personally? What about Tristen? He was a competitor, right?" I asked.

Shepherd grinned at Carlson. "Does this girl have a knack for questions or what?"

I lifted a shoulder. "I was there when it happened, and now I'm being personally attacked. I'd like to know who I'm facing."

He nodded. "Of course, but maybe you've missed your calling."

Amy answered my question. "Tristen Smith could buy and sell Hardcastle ten times over. There's nothing Hardcastle had that Tristen would want bad enough to kill over."

"What about the hacker Dennis Clark?" Carlson asked before explaining what had happened to my computer. "You know anything about him?"

"Other than what we all hear in the news when he pops some government email account? No, nothing personal. Hardcastle probably knew him, though. He knew everyone."

"So, do you have any ideas of who would tell Hardcastle the Madison Estate was for sale and set him up?"

They both shook their heads.

"Anyone who might use a boat to get to the property?" I asked.

Again he shook his head. "Especially not Tristen. He's notorious for his superstition of boats."

With that, they led us back out. I was disappointed as we headed to the car. Although I learned more about Hardcastle's marital affairs, we didn't get nearly as much information as I'd expected.

CHAPTER NINETEEN

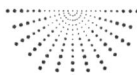

*C*arlson drove me back home. The sun had set, and evening settled in like a hen bustling down all cozy-like in her nest. He pulled in the driveway, and we kissed a few times, warm and gentle. I could tell he wanted to enjoy the moment for a while, but I couldn't get my head to stop spinning enough to relax. I patted his leg and hoped he'd forgive me.

I waved goodbye as he backed out, clutching the new burner phone we'd snagged at the gas station. Then his headlights swept away and I hugged myself and stared up at the first few night stars.

The light flicked on in the kitchen, creating a rectangle glow against the lilac tree. I wondered what Mom was up to. Where would we go when we had to leave here?

My thoughts spun in unhappy directions, and I sank into the porch swing with a thud. I pushed against the worn wood decking to start the swing and sent a text to Uncle Chris with my new phone number to reach me if he needed.

Then I returned to my thoughts about the lake at the house. What if the murderer hadn't come in by boat? Was it possible to swim that far? I had no idea, being a pretty horrible swimmer myself. I couldn't swim most of my childhood, no matter how hard my dad tried to teach me. Finally, he sent me to swimming classes, where a pimply-faced instructor with zero patience tried to teach me a few times. I'd been too scared, and the more he pushed, the more resistant I became. I may have inherited a bit of my Dad's stubborn streak.

Anyway, the kid came over in pretense to comfort me and ended up shoving me into the deep end. I sank under the water three times and was convinced I was about to die. But I ended up learning a weak doggy paddle. My fear of water grew to where I always claimed to want to "sunbathe" when my friends swam in the pool.

Years later, in teenaged bravado, I allowed someone to talk me into floating down the river like so many of my friends. That didn't end well either because the current dragged me over to where a tree had fallen into the water. I sailed straight for it with all those spiny branches poking straight at me.

All that meant I wasn't sure what really was possible in the water. The memories made me shiver, and I stared up at the sky. Clouds had rolled in and wrapped the stars and the rising moon in mists of storming threat.

The screen door screeched open.

"Honey, you're home?" Mom asked like she wasn't sure if I was ready to be disturbed or not.

"I am." I pushed with my toe again to keep the swing moving. The cushions were warm against my back. "Just thinking about all the crazy things I've learned today."

"Oh? Want some company?"

"Sure." I invited her over.

She came out to perch in a wicker chair, pulling her thin legs up and looking like she was twelve. It made me smile.

"Those birds are sweet, aren't they?" she said. "They can tell the rain is coming."

I nodded. "Yeah, you're right."

"I remember wanting to hear the rain so badly in jail. I missed the sound of it. I'd close my eyes and imagine it sometimes when I needed peace."

I winced. The trapped scene she described felt like it would drive me crazy.

Mom softly continued, "And you know, there's nothing you can do. The claustrophobia of being trapped with screaming women, fights over food, which step they wanted to sit on, women crying. The lack of hope. Sometimes I thought it would suck me under."

I stood up and crouched next to her chair and rested my forehead against her knee. I hated to hear this. Her words made my heart squeeze so tight.

"So I'd close my eyes and drape my arm over my face and pretend. 'I'll listen to the rain. I'll breathe.' I'd tell myself. And I'd pray. Sometimes we don't have the answer right now, but we still have to get through it. Even when all hope seems lost, God seems to give me something to hang on to."

"The rain."

"And my memories of you."

"Was it hard to think of me, knowing you couldn't see me?"

"There are two ways to think, and both lead to very different paths. One way is looking back and feeling like it's gone for good. The other way is to say this isn't permanent. There's always the possibility for change. I called that my God truth. And that's the path I usually took with my precious memories of you."

I blinked back the burn of tears.

"And look at us now." She softly stroked my hair.

"Love you, Mom."

"I love you too. More than you'll ever know." She leaned down to kiss my head. "Well, I have some chicken in the oven I better check. You like biscuits?"

I lifted my head. "I love biscuits."

"Good, I'll have some of those as well when you're ready." She patted my shoulder, and I scooted back so she could head inside.

The promised rain started to fall, lifting the humidity with its freshness. It spattered against the grass and mixed the sweet scent of its cleanness with the homey dinner inside. I almost laughed. What kind of crazy world was this? No mom growing up, but now she was making me dinner. I liked the unpredictable path of possibility and remembering there was always room for change.

The wind picked up and caused the trees to whisper with the raindrops' song. I pulled out the burner phone to check on something Shepherd had said. I wanted to know more about this little baby boy, now one of the wealthiest people in America.

First, I wanted to know when Marcus had been born. I checked the date of the boy's birth. Was it possible her son was late or early? Seven pounds eight ounces seemed right, but what did I know about these things?

The magazine announcement had pages of pictures showing the little family of three. Margaret looked surprisingly refreshed, and Marcus had the most gorgeous blue eyes I'd ever seen. They seemed very happy. Goes to show I couldn't judge happiness by a photograph. Proven by the fact Hardcastle had filed for divorce merely two weeks later.

I started a new search on Hardcastle. I found the same picture I'd seen earlier with the two realty moguls together. I remembered how Uncle Chris said they hadn't been together that day, and the image of the two together had been just a coincidence.

I zoomed in on the background. Carefully, I scanned all the dinner guests I could see.

This time I noticed someone. Andy sat at a background table. He had a phone in his hand, but his eyes were locked on Tristen.

Interesting. Was Andy there to have dinner as yet another random coincidence? Or was he there with Hardcastle?

Now I searched up Margaret. I found a gossip article about eleven months prior that showed a relaxed Margaret sitting at a poolside. That December, it seems she'd checked into Hyacinth Spa. I clicked the article and read about how both she and Hardcastle's assistant, Andy, were working on a cookbook she was in the middle of writing. It cracked me up to think of Andy being roped into writing a cookbook.

It also seemed odd that there was no mention of Hardcastle. Could this be an early sign there'd been trouble in paradise? They divorced a year later. Even if they didn't celebrate, it seemed couples typically wanted to spend holidays together.

I tried to find out where Hardcastle was that December. Nothing came up specific to that month, but I found an article with both Margaret and Hardcastle in front of a movie theater. The photo taken had been a closeup, and you'd never catch a hint of marital distress from their smiles.

I studied their picture again. And something struck me.

Something very obvious.

Both of their eyes were chocolate brown.

But I remembered how Marcus's were a startling blue.

Was this simply a case of a recessive gene? And, if so, whose gene was it?

CHAPTER TWENTY

This case was bananas. It felt like every string I pulled for an answer ended up unraveling more of my theory.

The rain stopped, and the only sounds were the little plops and splats falling from the trees.

I heard a weak meow and saw Gato poke his head out from under my car. His slick-backed hair framed his miserable eyes. He'd hid there when the storm started and had been trapped the entire time.

"Aww, buddy," I called.

The cat glanced my way with a decidedly dejected expression. I walked out to scoop him up. Smoothing his fur,

I carried him back to my swing and set him on the other cushion.

Apparently he was a great fan of this particular spot. I noticed orange hair covered the upholstery.

"Did you get stuck under there, buddy? Want to keep me company?"

He purred and licked his back furiously before curling up in a tight ball after adjusting a few times to get his feet and tail in just the right spot. I rubbed his cheek, feeling a bit sad. I only hoped the new people who moved in here would make good friends with him as I had.

Sighing, I looked back at my phone and pushed the swing. My next curious thought was about the results of the hospital fundraiser. My search brought up several, yet the hospital had only made it halfway to their goal. The biggest one had been a few weeks ago, a huge charity dinner. I clicked the media link for the photos of the fundraiser.

There were the usual suspects, the thin models and socialites all preening along the red carpet with one leg crossed over the other in front of the board. A few B celebrities all looking for exposure.

My eyebrows raised. And there was Tristen.

Interesting. Something struck me, and I flipped back to the previous picture. Was that Andy? I zoomed in. Sure enough, the young man stood in all lanky, awkward glory in the back of the crowd.

Why was the assistant to Mr. Hardcastle at a red carpet event?

I rose to my feet, tired and hungry. It had been a long day. Leaving Gato to happily snooze on the swing, I headed into the house where I found Mom in the kitchen peeling potatoes.

"What's up, buttercup?" she asked, using the pet name she'd had for me at five. "You look concerned."

I went to the fridge and searched for a soda. Popping the can open, I scooted onto one of the stools to watch her work. "Nothing really. I have a question for you, though."

"Hm?" I could see this pleased her. She loved needing to be needed. I was catching this sweet reciprocal mom/daughter relationship thing, and I adored it.

"It's about babies."

The peeler froze against the potato as her eyes flew wide. She didn't say anything but slowly looked up.

"Are all babies born with blue eyes, and when do they change color?"

She relaxed and leaned against the counter with a laugh.

"What?" I asked.

"Here, I thought I was rapidly graduating from being a mom to a grandma."

"What? Me?" Now it was my turn to laugh. "No, not for a while yet. I was thinking about Marcus."

"Who's Marcus?"

"He's Hardcastle's newborn son. He has the brightest blue eyes I've ever seen." Something hit me then... like a flickered memory. I couldn't track it down, so I dismissed it. "Anyway, both of his parents have dark brown eyes. I remember it can be a recessed gene, but it's not very common."

"Baby eye colors can change. But with a stark blue like you're describing, I'd be surprised if they turned brown."

"So a recessed gene then." I frowned. "Or—"

"Oh. Hm." Mom nodded and threw the peeled potato in the pot with a splash. She grabbed another.

"You know what I'm saying?"

"Sure. There's another baby-daddy."

I snorted. "Is that really a term?"

She shrugged. "Maybe. I have been out of the circuit for modern lingo for a while, though."

"Hardcastle might have suspected it. That was the reason his security guy, Shepherd, thought he might have filed for separation."

My phone rang then. My new one. I stared at it like it was a snake about to strike. Who had my number?

With the fear of the last phone call gripping my stomach, I answered, "Hello?"

"Stella, it's Carlson."

"Oh, hi!" I gushed in relief. "You'll never believe how scared I was just now to answer the phone. I thought—"

"Sorry to interrupt, but this is an emergency."

My blood felt like it turned into ice in my veins. "What's the matter?"

"It's you. I found out who called your phone earlier."

CHAPTER TWENTY-ONE

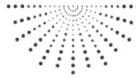

"Who?" I gasped. Mom obviously heard the panic in my voice and flicked a concerned glance at me.

"He goes by the name Masked Killer."

My adrenaline freak-out immediately halted with a loud, very unfeminine snort. "You're kidding me. Come on, Carlson. This isn't funny."

"Stella, I'm serious."

Masked Killer? Isn't he in some comic book?"

"Listen, dumb name or not, we don't know who he is. We know he likes knives. The important part you're not getting is that he knows who you are and how to reach you.

Detective Anderson is sending a car out to keep an eye out over your house."

That bit about knives straightened me right up. "Who is he? What does he look like? How do you know he's after me?"

I heard a long shaky exhale. "An anonymous call came in today to Detective Anderson, all of it pertaining to you. Only not so anonymous because he identified himself as the Masked Killer."

I stood up and started pacing. "Well, what do I do to stay safe? Go to a hotel? Hide out? What about my mom?"

Mom set down her paring knife and stared at me, her eyes wide.

"Right now, although the detective is taking this seriously, he's also cautiously optimistic that it's probably an empty threat. But I don't want you to count on that."

"Lovely," I said. All sorts of dangerous scenarios whipped through my mind with the fury of a tornado.

"Listen. I'm not trying to scare you, but I need you to be aware. This is the reality, at least for today. We're all working hard to change that reality."

I sighed. "Okay, double-checking the doors tonight. Hope I sleep."

"You'll see an officer drive by soon, I suspect. Hang in there. If anything suspicious happens, trust your gut and call someone."

"This is the second bigwig bad guy who's been after me. That's weird. Who am I that anyone would even care?"

"I don't have an explanation for that either, but I do know to stay on your toes regardless. They got to your computer, your phone, and now this threat. It doesn't have to make sense."

We said our mushy goodbyes, with mine being slightly more sentimental, spurred on by the vulnerability I now found myself in. And then I filled in Mom.

While she cooked, I stared at my phone. I should've felt scared. Maybe a part of me did. But as I sat here, second by second, another emotion grew.

Anger.

"Who are these people?" I growled and leaped off the stool to stalk into the living room. I flopped angrily into my overstuffed chair and pulled my laptop over.

Since my one solid lead in Erika Marsh pretty much evaporated, I needed to start over again. One more search on Hardcastle. The news was surprisingly bland, but he seemed well-favored by the public until the court case regarding the hospital. At that point, all the support and adoration he'd had in the past turned on a dime. The new headline screamed, "He hates all but the 1%!"

The following article portrayed the sale of the hospital in the most discouraging, depressing way. I could see why people had been against it.

I wished everyone could see the future and where we were now. Now the hospital was floundering, and the one person that might have been able to save the hospital— to give them a new beginning in a new building— happened to be murdered.

Margaret came up next on my list. I searched the Hyacinth Spa website, hoping to find a list of employees I might check with to see if Margaret had any visitors while she was there. Unfortunately, that went nowhere.

I returned to the activist Erika Marsh. She'd been my first lead. This time I noticed the hospital sale protests also happened that December. Could that be why Hardcastle hadn't been at the spa with his wife?

My mind went back to Tristen. And who the heck was Masked Killer? I wasn't sure if I wanted to look him up and read something that might freak me out more, so I put MK on the back burner.

I considered how in awe the computer repair guy had been about Dennis Clark. How strange that a hacker could be respected among the community.

Dennis lived in Australia. Yet he'd also recently visited our town at Tristen's Appaloosa Resort. He must have come all this way for a reason. And that reason couldn't have been to hack both Uncle Chris's and my computer.

So, if I was the afterthought, why had he really come?

I saw something out of the corner of my eye and jerked my head. A cop car slowly drove by, pausing for a moment before my driveway.

I sighed. I expected tonight would hold an interesting night's sleep.

"Dinner!" Mom called.

Truer words were never spoken. Mashed potatoes, roast chicken, and string beans waited for me in the kitchen.

It's funny how in some of the most challenging times, you could still find yourself with a monstrous appetite. Lovely didn't come close to describing the meal.

"Did you learn anything?" Mom asked, spooning up some gravy.

"Just more confusion about Hardcastle. And I don't understand why Dennis Clark traveled to the states."

She gave me a curious look, so I explained, "He's the cybercriminal who lives in Australia, but Uncle Chris discovered he'd traveled to our area recently. At a resort, actually."

"Oh, he probably was getting a massage. Detoxing."

Now it was my time to stare at her.

"I'm kidding." She smiled. "He obviously knows whoever owns the resort."

My mouth dropped, and then my fork to my plate. "You're a genius," I said and quickly pulled out my phone.

My memory served me well. Public records showed that Tristen's Barrington Towers Inc. owned the resort.

"So, you think Tristen was behind all of this? What would his motive be?"

I raked my fork through the mashed potatoes, creating an interesting shape. "Maybe he thought to scoop up the hospital at a cheap price if they went into foreclosure."

"Why didn't he then? You said Hardcastle lost the court case."

"I said it appeared he would lose. The case hasn't been settled yet. Maybe the tides were about to turn, and Hardcastle was on the brink of victory."

"Why not wait until the case finished, then?"

"I'm not sure. To be preemptive?" It didn't really make sense to me either. "Besides, if he did it, he must have hired someone else. Shepherd said he was terrified of boats and water."

"Because you think the killer came by water."

"Yeah, even though we couldn't find the landing spot."

"What about the dock?"

"It was in eyesight range the entire time. I would have seen someone there."

"Hmm," Mom hummed. It immediately dampened my enthusiasm for my new suspect.

"I can tell you have doubts, but why? He's the most obvious one. He can buy the hospital during foreclosure for a ridiculous price. The hacker was at his resort."

She stabbed her green beans. "That's my problem. He's so obvious. Someone with that kind of money would fly under the radar more. Not give red flags of motives everywhere they went."

"Isn't that how it goes with criminals?"

"Maybe the dumb ones. But the smart ones can hide a bit more. It's usually just one thing that's their undoing. A molehill. Not a whole heaping mountain."

I bit my thumbnail, thinking. "Actually, I have another problem. Tristen doesn't need the hospital, not even at a slashed price. Shepherd told me Tristen could buy and sell Hardcastle ten times over."

It was starting to feel like Tristen's motive was unraveling. Back to square one, my old friend. We meet again.

I saw a flash again as headlights reflected on my window. The officer drove by again.

"We have another problem, Mom," I said reluctantly. It was time to tell her what Mrs. Carmichael said.

"As long as we have each other, there aren't any problems," she responded to my terrible news.

"Seriously, we might have to find a new place to live. The landlord told me she will have to sell the place soon."

She shrugged. "It is what it is."

I felt guilty then. I was taking away the only home she'd known outside of prison, minus her experience twenty years ago. And now I'd unintentionally dragged her into a situation where someone was threatening me, and cops were driving by. I told her all this and then apologized. "I'm sorry, Mom."

She laughed and shocked me. "Stella, seriously. Life is crazy. But I've learned not to hang on to the physical quite so tightly. We'll be okay, I promise."

"But your home, Mom."

"Haven't you moved before?"

I nodded.

"Then you know that a house isn't the home. It's the people inside. Now eat your potatoes. They're getting cold. And I have apple crumble for later!"

CHAPTER TWENTY-TWO

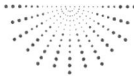

*T*hat night I slept like a baby. Which meant I woke up at regular intervals and never got more than a couple of hours of rest at a time. And, on my many trips to the bathroom, I'd stand before the window and stare out.

Now that the storm had passed, the full moon seemed especially large in the humid air. The light wrapped the front yard in its soft glow. The leaves on the stark tree branches barely moved. Once I saw the red taillights of the patrolling officer.

The next morning I felt wrung out like I'd run a marathon. I could barely keep my eyes open, exhausted and sweaty from nightmares and the lack of sleep, with my hair standing up like a toilet brush. Even a shower left me feeling only half-human.

The scent of bacon, however, perked me up considerably

I came down the stairs with my nose in the air to both sizzling and my mom humming. Those two sounds intermingling did my soul a whole lot better than a cup of coffee.

"Hi, Mom," I said upon entering. The cold floor bit my bare toes. I climbed up on a stool to tuck my feet on its rungs.

Mom spun around in surprise. "Hi, yourself, you scary lady."

I smiled, a little too pleased at the unintentional joke than I had a right to be for someone having their breakfast prepared for them. "Sorry for scaring you."

"It's that morning hair. Terrifying!" I laughed, and she added, "Want some coffee?"

"I can get it."

Before the words were out of my mouth, she put a mug under the maker and pressed start.

"Thanks," I said. "So, what are you doing today?"

"Probably more gardening. I found a patch of wild jumping-jacks that thrilled me. I might make lasagna for dinner."

I suddenly felt guilty at how bored she must be. "You can use my computer if you want. That might be fun."

"Oh, the internet. Thanks anyway, but I'm okay. From what I've seen, the internet is no real improvement for humanity."

"What do you mean?"

"I mean, sure, you have everything at your fingertips. But from my experience, humans need alone-time. It's where we are forced to sit with ourselves, think about what we really want and where we want to change. From what I've seen, the internet stops all that. It's a constant noise that never lets you think. And people easily get addicted to zoning out and not thinking."

I gave my laptop a suspicious stare. When she put it that way, I wasn't so sure about the time I spent on it myself.

"Well, how about coming with me today? You can hang out, and I'd like to show you the real estate office. See where I work, and the business Uncle Chris built."

"You sure? I don't want to trouble you. I can get along here."

"No, it'll be fun. Maybe we'll get a coffee or something."

"Okay," her voice sounded higher, girlish even. I could tell that made her happy. "Give me a few minutes to get ready."

Soon, we were on our way. She was suitably impressed when I pulled into the realty parking lot, with lots of oohing and ahhing over the giant pink flamingo on the sign. Of course, she wanted to know the story. I told her it was best told by Uncle Chris and we walked inside.

Kari wasn't there, which was a bummer, but Uncle Chris came out from his office to meet us.

"Vani! What do you think!" He gave her a big hug, nearly swallowing her in his arms.

"I love it, Chris. I'm so impressed."

He beamed like his favorite aunt showed up, and took a step back and glanced around the office like he was trying to see it with her eyes. His smile brightened when he saw the breakfast nook. "Come here! I have some doughnuts. Want some coffee?"

Right then, my office phone rang. At the same time, my new cell phone went off, sounding like a gargling bird. Caught between the two, I waved at Mom. "Go with him. I have to take these real quick."

With that, I dug for the cell as I ran for the office phone. Of course, it was too late by the time I got there. I had better luck with my cell and answered, a bit breathless, "Hello?"

"Hi Stella. It's Andy. Did I catch you at a bad time? You sound like you're exercising."

I laughed. "It feels like that sometimes when I try get my phone from my purse. Anyway, I'm not busy. What's up?"

"I have some paperwork I need you to sign. Mr. Hardcastle filled out a partial contract, and now it needs to get closed."

"Okay." I knew what he was referring to, but I had no idea it still mattered with Hardcastle deceased. "Do you want to fax it over?"

"Yeah, that will work. I'm heading out of town in a bit, and I'd like to get this off my plate."

"Sure. No problem. Send it over, and I'll get it done."

"Is your computer safe?"

"What do you mean?" I asked.

"You know…the hacker." His voice lowered like he thought the cybercriminal might be listening.

"Oh, him." Luckily Uncle Chris had come through with a new machine. "I have a new computer now. It's safe."

"So, you learn any more about Dennis Clark?"

"Not yet. How about you?"

"I did find something about who might have clued in Mr. Hardcastle to the fake pocket listing of Madison Estate."

"Really?" Sudden interest made me smile. "Who was it?" A pause grew on the other end. "Andy?"

"Listen, I'm not comfortable with how your computer was hacked. For all I know, your office is bugged as well. This is kind of...sensitive information. I don't want it coming back to bite me."

"Of course. I understand." I bit my thumbnail in frustration.

"Listen, how about if we meet at Lakebay? I'll be driving down that way in about four hours. Would that be too late to grab a cup of coffee? We can talk, and I'll fill you in. You can sign the paperwork and bring me the hard copies. That would work better for me, anyway."

I considered it for a second. Lakebay was a bit of a drive.

"I really think you need to know this," he urged. "Besides...coffee."

I remembered how his card had been denied last time and wondered if I'd be paying again. Still, all in all, it seemed a small price for some information. "You got it. I'll see you later this afternoon."

With the plan set in motion, we said goodbye. I glanced at Mom, who was over in the corner, doughnut in one hand and a cup of coffee in the other. She nodded like her head was on a spring while Uncle Chris talked a mile a minute.

I knew how energetic his conversations could be. With a wry grin, I called Carlson.

"Hey, Hollywood. Whatcha doing? Things stay safe and quiet last night?"

"Not a creature was stirring," I said. "Except for the cop who drove by every so often. Overall, the only interesting thing that happened was my nightmares."

"Aw, hard night sleep, huh? I'm sorry."

"That's what coffee's for," I said. "How about you?"

"I'm working, but I'll be done tonight. You have plans?"

"Andy just called my cell. He wants me to sign a contract closed. He really puzzled me."

"Why is that?"

"Well, he asked me about Dennis Clark. I can't remember talking to Andy about him."

"Strange. You think you just don't remember?"

I have been distracted lately. "Yeah, probably. I guess I'm second-guessing everything."

"Hey, I appreciate that about you. You like to ask questions and dig a little. I love you just the way you are."

Silence prickled between us. Neither one of us had used the "L" word yet. I waited for him to take it back, to turn it into a joke. Something.

There was nothing there but his quiet confidence. I really admired that about him. But I wasn't ready to respond in the same way.

Gently, I changed the subject. "We're a good team. We can question things together."

He let me shrug it off. "Maybe dinner tonight?"

"Yeah, maybe."

"Burgers?"

Normally that would be a yes, but not today. "Meh," I answered.

"Tacos?" he tried again.

"Not today."

"How about seafood? I know a great place that has seafood fettuccine and garlic butter clams by the bucket."

"I didn't know you liked shellfish."

"Oh, you bet I do. I can pick you up and take you to the Fisherman's Wharf. Sound good?"

"Maybe," I hedged. I was really indecisive today.

"Come on. We'll get some crab as well. It's been ages since I've had that."

"Okay, see you tonight."

CHAPTER TWENTY-THREE

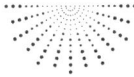

I searched my email, waiting for Andy's contract. From across the room, I heard Mom finally get a word in with a soft-spoken question about the origin of the flamingo. Uncle Chris heartily laughed and brought out the story of race cars and a lost bet.

Finally, Andy's e-document showed up. I quickly filled out my part and sent it to the printer.

I glanced at Uncle Chris and Mom and knew I could go join their conversation. But I was reluctant to give up trying to figure out who murdered Hardcastle. If not Erika, and not Tristen, then who could have a motive?

As a last resort, I typed in Margaret Hardcastle. Was she grieving or relieved her ex-husband was dead? I organized the news stories by most recent and found an article saying she was staying yet again at the Hyacinth spa.

I guess she was doing her own version of chilling out. But what about her baby? Maybe her parents had the little guy.

That wasn't the only thing that came up about her. I saw another photo tagged with her name. In it she was making a similarly angry face that had made Kari crack up the first time. It was posted by a gossip site with the question, "What Red Apple power couple might now be headed to divorce with an air-tight prenup after discovering there may have been an affair? And one that definitely fathered a child."

It made me think of a comment Andy once said about how Tristen owned a famous NYC apartment building and another two hundred more. Quickly, I checked to see who owned the spa.

Barrington Towers Incorporated.

Jackpot! My jaw dropped, and I scrambled to search for a picture of Tristen. I found the one of Hardcastle and Tristen at the Philadelphia restaurant. Tristen's blue eyes were startling. Blue like the baby's. Was it possible that Hardcastle was not there as a coincidence but to confront Tristen?

I clicked on yet another picture, and my hope deflated a bit. Taken at yet another red carpet event of the opening of his newest building, Tristen was dressed to the nines. His hand rested familiarly on the elbow of a beautiful young lady.

Okay. Don't freak out. So what if Tristen had a girlfriend. He still could have fathered a child with Margaret, right?

Just then, Mom showed up at my desk. She carried a few boxes in her hands. "Chris wondered if we could drop these off at the post office."

I checked the time and pushed away from the computer. "Sure. And after we'll grab a coffee from my favorite place." I realized then I'd forgotten about the lasagna with my newly-made lunch plans with Andy. And then I had plans with Carlson! What had I been thinking?

"Mom, I'm sorry, but I have to cancel our plans tonight. I have a business meeting for lunch, and then Carlson called and invited me to dinner. I forgot about our lasagna and said yes. I can postpone with him if you want."

She smiled, relaxed. "Honey, that's fine. I mean, it's really your loss since I make the best lasagna ever." She winked at me. "Seriously, I'll make it another time.

Even with her reassurance, I felt terrible.

"I'm sorry again." I gave her a hug. "But we'll have fun today. Come on, let's go. And when we get back, Kari might be here. She's a hoot."

We headed straight to the post office where I ran inside to drop off the packages.

The next stop was at my darling Darcie's Doughnuts. Mom sniffed appreciatively when we walked in. Chocolate, vanilla, fried heavenly goodness, I couldn't get enough.

"Stella! Yoohoo!" called a cheery voice. I turned and saw the Valentine sisters. Charity and Gladys were both somewhere in their early eighties, and I'd helped sell their family manor when I first moved here. They couldn't be more opposite of each other. Gladys towered over me ramrod straight, hair pulled in a tight bun, and stern glasses to match her stiff smile. Charity was as round as a button, hair amok with curls, and she hardly came to my collar bone. It was Charity who called me now.

"Hi!" I gave her a smile. "How are you?"

That wasn't good enough for her. She ran over and gave me a big hug. I felt the love and hugged her back.

"Laura Lee." Gladys stared down her nose at me. "I hope you're well."

"I'm good, thank you," I answered.

"And who is this?" Charity stared expectantly at my mom with shining eyes.

"This is Vani, my mom."

"Oh!" squealed Charity. "I'm so happy to meet you. You are this girl's momma? She's the best. We just love her."

"Love's a strong word," sniffed Gladys. "I'd save that for cherub angels of the supernatural sort."

"And Valentines!" giggled Charity. "Which we are." She grasped Mom's outstretched hand and pumped it. "I truly am so pleased to meet you."

"Likewise," my somewhat stunned mother answered back.

"I heard all about that horrid officer and the false imprisonment. You poor dear." Charity patted my mother's arm.

Even Gladys seemed to appear sad. "Most regretful."

"Well, I'm enjoying being out now. There's no looking back and today has a lot to be grateful for." Mom's eyes grew a little misty.

"There, there. And you deserve every bit of happiness. Why, you're back with your daughter now. I can't believe it's taken this long to meet. Shame on Stella for keeping you locked away." Charity smiled.

Mom and I glanced at each other at her awkward terminology.

Gladys tried to cover. "So, what have you been doing up at that small house?"

"My latest passion is being able to get back into gardening. I used to have a neighborhood garden way back when. It's amazing to get back into it."

Charity didn't notice her little faux pas. She clapped her hands. "You know how to do bucket gardens? Gladys, I think this is our answer!"

"What answer?" Mom asked.

Charity calmed down as if she didn't want to scare my Mom away. "I work at a lovely assisted living home in town. Our residents are some of the most delightful people you've ever met. I've been looking for something for them to do, and some are just craving to get their hands in the dirt. Green thumbs, you know. They've been doing it their whole lives. I think having a pot with a few carrots or maybe a little green pepper — "

"Potatoes grow well," Mom suggested.

"Yes, maybe on the grounds we could have a barrel of those," Charity mused, her eyes taking on a far-away expression.

"Anyway," Gladys prodded.

Charity beamed at my Mom. "And I think you would be the perfect person to lead us in that endeavor. It would be paid, of course. And you could make your own hours. Our residents are early risers, so there is that."

"Paid?" I asked Charity.

"Didn't you know? I'm the activity director there now." Charity beamed.

Somehow Charity had taken a volunteer position and turned it into something paid. All I knew was that the nursing home made a good decision seeing the treasure they had in Charity.

My cell rang with its scary warped bird ringtone. I dragged it out of my purse to answer.

"Stella? It's Andy. I'm sorry, but can we meet sooner? I ended up finishing ahead of schedule, and I'd like to get an early start back to the city."

I hesitated and stared at Mom.

"What is it?"

"Just one second, Andy." I hit mute. "It's about the business meeting. He wants to meet earlier."

"Oh?"

"Like now. He has to leave again in an hour."

"Oh." There was a decided note in the last response. We both realized the length of the return trip home.

"Well," Mom continued. "Why don't you leave me here? I can take a nice walk—"

I shook my head.

Charity jumped in. "Don't be silly! We'd love to take you home. And we can talk more about the art assistant we need at the nursing home. Maybe we can talk her into it yet!"

I glanced at Mom and silently checked to see if she'd be okay. Mom grinned and waved me off. "You go on ahead. It seems I have a lot to discuss. I'll see you at home."

"Keep the doors locked," I warned. "Call me."

"Yes, Mom," she said with a sassy wink.

I rolled my eyes and unmuted Andy.

"Hey, Stella," he answered.

"I can do it!"

"Great. I'm on my way now."

CHAPTER TWENTY-FOUR

*A*s I jogged to my car, I saw I had a message from Carlson. —**Looking forward to tonight!**

Smiling, I texted back—**Me too! Andy called to move the meeting up, so I'm on my way. And my new phone has a weird ringer! Sounds like a parakeet! LOL**

I waved at Mom, who peered through the bakery window, and then I was off for the lake.

With the light traffic, the drive to Lakebay passed rather pleasantly, and it didn't seem long at all before I pulled into the Lakebay parking lot. The remote park was predictably empty because of a giant berm that hid it from the highway. Most people didn't even know it was here.

I spotted Andy's car as the only vehicle in the lot—minus a broken-down van in the corner that probably was stolen—and pulled in next to it.

I climbed out, slid on my sunglasses, and scanned the area. There was a building near the shore. The water splashed lightly against the beach while the lake rippled with little white dots of sunlight.

Andy came out of the building and stared in my direction. He waved, which I returned happily as the balmy breeze caressed my bare arms, bringing back the feeling of summer vacation. I strode down across the soft sand toward him.

"Hey, you," I called. The sun warmed my face, and I tipped my head back to enjoy the rays. "How did you know I was here?"

"Heard the car door slam. Long time no see."

The wind ripped at his button-up shirt that he'd left untucked from his pants. The first three buttons were undone as well. A baseball cap sat on his head.

"You doing better?" I asked. As I closed in, I saw that he had a bit of a tan. And was that a smile?

"Never better. You get the contracts?"

"Yep. Here they are." I pulled the envelope from my handbag where I'd tucked the paperwork and handed it to him. He slid the envelope into the back pocket of his jeans.

"Thanks. Glad that's over with." He stared out at the lake. "The water's beautiful. You been here before?"

"Not really. I've only driven by."

He scuffed the sand with his shoe. I was surprised he'd foregone the business loafer and wore a pair of sneakers. "This was my stomping ground when I was in high school. Used to hang out at that rock over there. We'd drink in there at night." Here he jabbed a thumb in the direction of the little building.

We walked together along the shoreline. I felt increasingly curious why he'd called this meeting. He didn't say anything, so I started with my questions.

"Have you learned anything more about Hardcastle's death?"

"Other than we barely escaped with our lives? And that someone is listening?"

I gasped. "Have you been targeted, too?"

"What do you mean?"

"Well, like you mentioned, my computer had been hacked." Something hit me then. "How did you know about that?"

"Oh, your uncle told me."

Something about that didn't sit right with me, but I accepted it for the moment.

He continued. "I had a weird thing happen with the emails. Just like what happened to you. Every single email that pertained to the Madison Estate all disappeared."

"Wow! Are you getting any strange phone calls?"

"Strange phone calls? No, nothing."

"How am I so lucky?" I said, half to myself.

"You must make an impression on people. You have that charismatic personality."

I snorted. "Nobody's ever told me that before."

"Trust me. Unforgettable."

I squinted at him. Was he hitting on me? Quickly, I changed the subject. "So, I have a theory."

A seagull swooped over head with a squawk. We both looked.

Andy continued, "What's that?"

Here it goes. "For a while, I thought Tristen killed Hardcastle."

He snorted. "Why would he do that? Trust me, their rivalry for real estate never went that deep."

"You're right. Tristen had more money than he knew what to do with. There's nothing Hardcastle had that he needed.

Except for one thing. Love. Tristen loved Margaret. I think they had a kid together."

"What are you talking about? There's only Marcus. The kid's only two months old." Andy raised his eyebrows in confusion.

"Exactly." I nodded.

"Come on, Stella. That's pretty drastic. Why not just divorce?"

"The prenup assured she received nothing. And in case of Hardcastle's death, the law says all estate is divided between wife and child."

"So they divorced."

"Right, but they still were dealing with child custody. Hardcastle wanted a paternity test. So that would have ruined everything. But I think my theory's garbage now."

"Geez, you're bouncing like a tennis ball. Why the change?"

"I found a picture with Tristen and his girlfriend."

"Really?" He sounded surprised. "Where was that?"

"At the grand opening of his newest building."

Andy hesitated.

"What?" I asked. His forehead wrinkled in indecision. "What?" I repeated.

"I hate to encourage your theory in any way, but that woman is Clarissa. She's his sister."

"Wait, what?" His sister! Hope hit me again that I might be on to something. But why had Andy been so hesitant?

"Yeah. It's true," he said.

I gazed at the water. A tiny sailboat rode the breeze with its sails full and white with the wind's swell. "You know what this means, right?"

"I do."

"This puts Tristen back in the forefront."

"You think so?" He adjusted his glasses, in the process knocking his hat off. As he ran to chase it, I saw we were no longer alone on the beach. A man was out walking.

It hit me then how, when I'd arrived, Andy said he'd heard my car door shut. He was in a building with waves on the lake making a soft sound. Essentially the same situation I'd been at Madison Estate. The house wasn't that large nor especially soundproof, and the Range Rover had been just outside.

Why hadn't I heard the Range Rover's door shut when we were in the house?

Andy's phone rang, and he pulled it from his pocket to answer it. "Hello?" His tone flattened, and his Adam's apple sharply bobbed as he swallowed. After listening, he turned away from me and quietly said, "I just need a little more time."

He hung up. His face had drained of blood, now a shade of thin milk.

"Who was that? Are you okay?" I asked, concerned.

He stared at me then. There was something odd about his expression.

CHAPTER TWENTY-FIVE

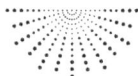

*M*y cell phone rang then. I kept my eyes on Andy as I searched for it. Annoyingly, it rattled around somewhere at the bottom of my purse. I dug around, my fingers slipping across lipstick, a brush, tissues, pens, finally grabbing the vibrating irritation.

As I answered it, I heard someone behind me say, "Hello, Stella."

I spun around to see the man from the beach now walking toward me. Something about his voice seemed familiar.

I brought the phone to my ear.

The man waved at me then, and my gaze landed on a shiny thing in his hand. A pistol. Snub-nosed and pointed straight at me.

He shook his head. "I wouldn't do that if I were you."

All the words I'd been planning to speak into the phone froze like an ice cube caught in my throat. My hand with the phone stayed locked by my ear.

"Stella?" Carlson's frantic voice blasted through the speaker. "Stella, something's wrong. How did Andy have your new phone number to call you? It was brand new and unlisted. I don't have a good feeling about this. Don't go to that meeting."

The gun wavered before me. I didn't move a muscle.

"Hang up," said the man. I realized then that this was the same person who called me on the phone.

My pulse hammered in my ears. Slowly, I lowered my arm.

"Come on, we don't have all day." The man gestured with his pistol.

"Stella?" yelled Carlson, just as I jabbed the end button with my thumb.

My tongue didn't want to move, but I needed to make a show of confidence. "Do I know you?"

"I'm not sure. Probably. After all, you've been looking for me for a few days now."

"I have?"

The man smiled then, and his features fell into place. I hadn't recognized him at first from the pictures online.

Bright blue eyes and perfect teeth. Tristen.

"Andy, run!" I yelled and threw my purse at Tristen.

Tristen batted it away with a laugh. "Yes, Andy. Run. Run as fast as you can."

I glanced over at Andy. He hadn't moved. Instead, his fingers twisted together nervously. He caught my eye for a mili-second before his gaze dropped away as he reached to shove up his glasses.

"Andy?' I asked, half-whispered.

He looked away. "I just needed more time," he hissed. I realized then he was speaking to Tristen.

"Ahh, you're figuring it out," Tristen announced with a hearty smile. It freaked me out. "Finally, things are coming together. I bet that feels good. Yes, I needed someone close to Hardcastle to get the, as they say, the *job* done. Obviously, I couldn't ask you. But I could use you to be a *great* witness."

It came to me then. Two thoughts butting into one another. The first was something Andy had said the day Hardcastle had been murdered. "When you have that kind of money, you don't do it yourself. You hire someone." And the second compliments of Carlson. "Because someone thinks you're the perfect Patsy, maybe."

Tristen spelled it out as clear as day. "I hired Dennis Clark to hook both Hardcastle and your Uncle Chris with a little email bait about a pocket listing, and a request that you be there. And then I hired Andy to close the deal."

I looked at Andy in shock. "Why would you?"

He half-heartedly shrugged. "The guy was stingy. It's not fun having your credit card always declined."

"His name was Hardcastle. Not guy," I reminded Andy. And then in disbelief. "You killed him?"

He shrugged. "I did it prior to your arrival. He was long gone before we ever entered the house."

That's why I didn't hear the killer open Hardcastle's door to kill him. "And the gunman? The panic? You were just acting?" It was insane, but I needed more confirmation.

"I'm pretty good, aren't I?"

I felt sick to my stomach. I turned to Tristen. "So, you're Marcus's real father."

"Did my blue eyes give me away?"

"That and the fact that she stayed at your spa."

Tristen shrugged. "You're not as dumb as you look. Pretty dumb, though, to be out here with us. Especially after I called to threaten you as the infamous Masked Killer." He chuckled at his own joke.

"I'm not dumb. I trusted him," I said defensively with a fierce stare at Andy.

"Well, didn't your Mom ever tell you that you can't trust people you don't know?"

I jerked, startled. Did he know more about me than I realized? Or was this a flippant comment?

His wavering pistol reminded me it didn't matter now. I needed to figure a way out of this mess.

"Should we go for a walk?" Andy nodded toward the boat shack.

"I don't want to go for a walk," I said. My muscles felt like I'd fallen off an iceberg. I wasn't sure I could get them to move.

"He wasn't asking. Come on. Let's go." Tristen roughly grabbed my arm and yanked me forward.

I glanced at the parking lot, willing someone to pull in. I could hear the highway over the dirt bulkhead. It was infuriating to be so close to help and so far away.

I had to do something. My purse lay uselessly on the ground, spilling out any other possible weapon. I only had on sneakers, the thick rubber soles making them the worst things to be wearing to kick someone.

My panic rose. I shot a pleading glance at Andy. "Please," I whispered. "You don't have to hurt me. I'll go. No one will know."

"Know what, sweetheart?" Tristen asked. "Know that I fathered Marcus? We definitely don't want that getting out. As it stands, the little man stands to inherit Hardcastle's entire estate."

"Don't you have enough?" I asked. "Aren't you like one of the richest men in the United States?" I glared at Andy for betraying me. How I'd like to get my hands on him now.

"I'm a bigger fish than that, sugar. But never look a gift horse in the mouth. And that's what this is. I'll marry Margaret. And the three of us will have a fabulous time."

I'd slowed my pace, but he noticed and yanked my arm. He continued his soliloquy. "A grand old time. For a couple of years at least."

Andy smirked as he shuffled beside us.

"Then it will be time to play the grieving widower. What do you think, Andy?"

"Sounds like a plan to me." Andy pushed up his glasses.

"And then we'll be working on a new mama for little Marcus."

"You're sick," I muttered, dragging my feet.

Tristen laughed. "Come on. Let's go."

CHAPTER TWENTY-SIX

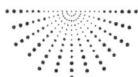

*T*wo thoughts raced through my mind. The first — Carlson's going to kill me — maybe Oscar too since I'd promised I would never get in this type of situation again.

The second was far darker. You can't kill what's already dead.

I glanced up the beach, but we were alone.

My foot rolled on a pile of stones, and I nearly fell over. Tristen's hand pinched my arm tighter.

"Ow," I muttered.

"Keep your step and move those feet," he muttered back.

"Why are you doing this? It makes no sense."

"Why? Why wouldn't you let well enough alone? The last thing I needed was for you to go with your little theory to your boyfriend. It would all be over."

My mouth dried like talcum powder. "How did you know?"

"Oh, Dennis is a dream. He found your linked iCloud account to your phone, and we've been watching it ever since. Every keystroke, every search. Every text. Chris as well. How do you think we got your new number?"

It made me sick that I'd missed the fact that Andy had called my number. My distractions about finding Hardcastle's killer did me in, and made me miss something so obvious. Missed the trees for the forest, or so they say. I stared up at the shack. I knew I couldn't let him take me there, nor on the dock. It was too out of sight. I truly could disappear forever.

My heart hammered out the correction, would, not could.

I had to try to break away. There was nothing for it. At the next pile of stones, I let myself slip, pitching sideways with my full weight.

I slipped out of his grip and landed hard on the ground. "Ow!" I yelled, grabbing my ankle. I didn't have to act.

"Get up," he demanded.

Real tears squeezed out of my eyes, half from fear and pain. "I can't. I think I broke it."

Tristen sighed in disgust. "Get her." He waved the gun at me.

Andy stood back. "What?"

"Get her! Help her! Pick her up. Do something!"

"I can't pick her up."

"You were strong enough to shove a blade through a man's chest for money. I'll give you more money. Just pick her up. We have to get out of here."

"Why?" Andy walked over to me, looking as wimpy as a noodle. "Just do it here."

"It's not isolated enough. Someone might hear us. Now get her."

Andy came over to grab my arm. I reached for his and gave it a mighty pinch.

"Ow, you—" He brought his fist back as if to hit me, and I screamed and ducked.

"Enough!" Tristen hollered. He rolled his eyes. "I swear I have to do everything around here." He reached down and yanked me to my feet. "Come on."

He dragged me along. This time, Andy trailed behind. I glanced back and saw a bitter look in his eye. He rubbed the spot where I pinched him.

Tristen hauled me over driftwood. We were nearly there. It was almost too late.

I slowed again, and this time Andy shoved me from behind. I went flying. My knees smartly smashed against the pebbly beach.

"Hey! When I ask for your help, do something," Tristen yelled, frustrated. He yanked me to my feet again.

"Let me take care of her. I owe her for this." Andy rolled up his shirt sleeve to show a bright blue bruise.

Tristen laughed. "She gave you a little kiss, did she? I suppose you owe her one back. But not until we get into the beach house."

I made up my mind then. I'd throw myself off the dock and try to take cover under the wood before he started firing his gun. They could jump after me, it was true. I'd handle that when it happened. I could only do one step at a time.

We were almost there now. The planks were just before us. I took a deep breath, trying to be subtle. Who knew how long I'd have to hold my breath. I could do this. I sucked in a breath and stared at the dock.

"Well, at least she's cooperating," noted Tristen. "I want to reward her."

"You promised me," complained Andy.

"As long as she complies, we won't make her suffer. That's a good deal, right, little one?"

I hated his nickname. The only point was to lull me into a sense of security.

I had about as much of a safety guarantee as Hardcastle did. And Margaret, assuming I lived from this.

We stepped onto the dock. This one floated as well. The waters were rougher here, and the dock bobbed like a fishing lure. I stared down at the water. Seaweed-like plants floated on its surface. Underneath was something murkier. Something I was going to meet in just a minute. I hoped.

"This the best place you could find?" Tristen complained.

"You asked me for someplace remote on the fly. It was all I could think of without some searching," Andy answered defensively.

"Let me guess. You partied here as a teenager." Tristen kicked a beer can.

Andy ignored him, but I swear I felt him shrivel.

Breathe in deep. Hold it. Look for your opportunity.

I felt it then. Tristen's grip on my arm lessened slightly. He tried to catch his balance as he was on a board behind me. I stepped ahead to get on the up bobble as he stayed on the down one.

How deep was the water here? Deep enough? Waist deep? I needed it over my head. I also had to go when I had a chance. Would the two moments collide?

Deep breath. Get ready to hold it. Any second.

Tristen clamped down on my arm. "Hold it right there, missy. Don't be too eager now."

He yanked me back toward him. My heart sank when he adjusted his hand to have a better grip. "Come here. What are you running off for?"

We were nearly at the end of the dock. It was now or never.

Deep breath. Don't give up.

Just then, Andy staggered on the dock. He misjudged the footing and stepped wrong, stumbling as the dock melted from under his foot.

"Son of a—" he screamed.

I didn't hear the rest of it. At that moment, I wrenched my arm from Tristen's grasp and dove into the water.

Icy cold water wrapped around me like a death shawl. Shock hit me for a second, making me want to react with a gasp. I held it together and kicked my legs.

In the next few moments, I made it under the dock. I tried to come up, hoping and praying for just an inch of clearance so I could take a breath.

Up I came, eyes squeezed shut. My face bumped into the wood.

Still under water.

My eyelids popped open. I saw a streak of bubbles. Someone up there was shooting. My heart squeezed, but I couldn't let myself think about it. I kicked and reached out for the shallow end.

By a miracle, this end had a tiny pocket between the water and the wood. I shoved my face against the boards and gasped for air. Too late, I realized I needed to breathe quietly.

"She's down here!" I heard a scream. I dunked my head under and moved closer to the beach. When I came up again, I purposely breathed quieter.

"Where is she? You see her?"

"I can't believe you bumped into me and knocked my hand off her," Tristen snarled.

I straightened my body. I could reach the lake floor here. Water hit me in the face, and I swallowed.

"You see her?"

A shot blew through the dock, the bullet spiraling through the water. A clear dot of light shone through the wood deck.

"Stop it! You want to alert someone?"

"I thought I saw her!"

"You can't keep popping those off." Tristen admonished. That meant Andy had a gun as well. Two pistols. Horrifying.

I crept along the dock. The water became shallower and shallower. It ended in a muddy bank. Finally, my shoes might be of use. I dug into the sand, hoping to create a hollow I could hide inside.

"What do we do?" Andy asked.

"Get in there. Jump!"

My heart froze. What was I going to do when he confronted me under here?

"You want me to jump in the water?"

"Did I stutter? Get in there!"

Okay. I had no time to freak out. I needed to think of my next defensive move. The dirt stirred in the water from my digging. I wouldn't be able to see a rock, no matter how hard I tried. Besides, every movement underwater was clumsy as if my limb weighed a thousand pounds.

I stared up at the boards. Could I break one off?

I hardly dared to try, afraid my fingertips would be visible on the deck above.

They argued some more. "You know how cold the water is? She probably has hypothermia by now."

"Get. In."

Lucky for me, Andy's guess about the water temperature was incorrect. But not too far off. Right now, my adrenaline kept me warm. Still, the icy cold bit through my clothes. A leaf floated in my face, and I swatted it away.

My hand came across a root or piece of driftwood buried in the bank under the dock. I quickly worked to free it.

"Now!" screamed Tristen.

I yanked hard and the root came free. I took another deep breath to prepare to duck under the water to watch. My next plan would be to try and move up the bank. There was nothing for cover, though. Nothing.

Don't think about that now. Breathe deep and concentrate.

As I breathed in, I heard something else. It came from far away. I might have dismissed it as a hallucination rather than force my brain to decipher the words. But it was so odd, I forced myself to focus.

"Stop right there. You're under arrest."

As their meaning came into focus I realized they were the most beautiful words in the world. Better than any melody I'd ever heard.

"Who are you?" asked Tristen.

"He's—"

"Officer Carlson, and you have one second to toss the guns and get those hands up."

I couldn't imagine how he found me.

"Now!" he screamed. I heard two clunks on the boards above me. "Good, now come toward me. Slowly."

Thumps and footfalls traveled toward me. Debris fell on my upturned face as they walked over me.

"Get on your knees," Carlson demanded. At this point, I couldn't hear more because of the water slapping the underside of the pier. Minutes passed, and I wondered if I could safely come out. Water splashed my face, or maybe they were tears. I couldn't tell at this point.

Then I heard him scream, "Where is she?"

I crept along the side of the bank, the water pulling on my legs as I gripped the slimy rocks. As it became shallower, I poked my head out from under the pier. "I'm here!" I yelled.

"Stella?" Carlson turned in my direction, his face white and his eyes tense with emotion.

Slowly, I dragged myself up the bank. He ran over to help me, leaving both Andy and Tristen on their faces with their hands cuffed behind their backs. He half heaved me out and pulled me into his arms. His muscles trembled.

"How did you find me?" I gasped.

"I installed the find your phone app just in case."

"Always so smart." My legs began to shake, and he held me firmly. In the background, sirens approached.

"Listen, next time, if you want to get out of having seafood with me, just let me know. We'll find a different restaurant. No need for all these dramatics," he muttered into my wet hair.

My teeth chattered. "You said you loved me just the way I was."

"You got that right, Hollywood." And he squeezed me tighter.

CHAPTER TWENTY-SEVEN

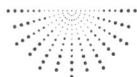

$\mathcal{T}$wo weeks had passed since the confrontation at the lake. More news came in about Andy. It seems that Tristen had met Andy during the time Margaret stayed at his spa. Andy had been with her, helping to write her cookbook. Tristen saw how desperate Andy was for money. After doing a little digging, it came up that the young man had massive student loans, a car repo, and more.

Apparently, Andy was willing to do anything to get out from under debt and live a life of luxury. Tristen exploited that desire and hired him to take out Hardcastle. Margaret maintained her innocence that she knew nothing about it. I hoped, for the sake of her son, that this was true.

Dad had not taken the news well to say the least. Between a three-way phone call with Mom and myself and a lot of patience, he finally calmed down. Still, I think that influenced his decision to move his vacation up a few weeks. He was on an airplane at the moment and due to land any minute.

Mom and I relaxed in the porch swing as we waited for him to show up. The sun had set hours ago, and the stars sparkled like a child's glitter project on black construction paper.

"You excited?" I asked.

"I really am. Did you know your dad's thinking of retiring soon?"

"I did. Maybe by then he'll realize I'm an adult."

"I might have missed a lot of your growing up, but I've always known you're daddy's little girl. He'll probably continue to think of you that way even when you're a grandma."

"He's always been the best dad."

"I know. I picked him, you realize." She laughed.

I pushed gently, my head resting on the back of the swing.

"Look at those." Mom pointed.

I lifted my head to see and then smiled. "My little star warriors."

"You would call them that. Back where I'm from, they're called lightning bugs."

"Really? Not fireflies?"

"Nope. And we call coke, soda pop."

"How funny." I rested my head again. "You know, I don't know anything about your family."

She stared as if at something particular. In reality, I could see she was watching memories being played out in her head. "Unfortunately, my family's been gone for a long, long time. I think that's why I glommed on to Oscar so hard when I married your dad. That internal hunger for a father." Her gaze quickly met mine. "You know, no matter what evidence they presented in the trial, he never believed it. He always saw me as innocent and put money on my books while I was in there."

I believed it. "He kept an eye out for me growing up as well."

She nodded. "I know. He sent me pictures and updates."

"He did?" This pleased me immensely.

A shy smile crept over her lips. "And I was extremely proud of you. Always."

Tears burned my eyes. I blinked like I was in a cloud of campfire smoke.

"That's interesting you bring that up. Actually, there's something I wanted to share with you." She shifted slightly. "You know how my grandmother immigrated over here from Poland.

I nodded. "Dad gave me letters from her."

"You have them?"

"Yep!"

Now it was her turn to look especially pleased. "Your dad saved them for me while I was gone."

"I'll get them for you when we go inside."

"Well, the thing is, I received a letter, myself. Years ago in jail." Mom said. "It caught me off guard. So much so, I didn't know what to think and stuffed it away."

"What did it say? Was it a threat?" My tone rose with my anger.

She shook her head. "No. In fact, I saved it. I always meant to follow up with it one day when, if, I ever got free." Her cheeks colored at the last word. It said so much. This was a woman who held onto the dream that maybe one day she would be free, despite being convicted for a crime she didn't commit.

That was hope right there.

"What did it say?" I asked.

"Well, if we can't stay here, I might have an adventure to take. You could come with me if you wanted." She stood up. "Let me go get it."

When she returned she held a letter from a business envelope. The paper had that worn look of having been folded and refolded many times.

"This is from a prawnik."

"A what?"

She laughed. "Otherwise known as a jurist or lawyer. It's about my great grandparents."

"Really? I'd read the letters Wiktoria had sent her mom back at home."

"Oh, good. Long story short, there's a family home over there. It seems I'm the last living relative."

My jaw dropped. "Seriously?"

She nodded. "What do you think? You want to explore Poland with me? And maybe Dad. We'll see about that retirement of his."

I felt too shocked to respond. Seconds ticked by while the tiny cogs of my brain turned to digest this information. "I think so. I never thought about visiting Poland before."

"You'll love it. It's a gorgeous country—rich in history."

I smiled then. Life sure kept the surprises coming, didn't it? I didn't know if I could actually take the time off to go or not, but it was sure fun to think of the possibilities.

"Mom, I'm honored you would ask me. Let me think about it."

"Sure. There's no rush."

Just then, headlights turned into the driveway. Dad was here. I started to stand to greet him when I noticed Mom had. Casually, she stepped down the stairs and walked toward him as he climbed out of the car.

The moonlight softened his features. I noticed he walked toward her rather than immediately get the suitcases out like he always had before.

"Hi," Mom said.

"Vani, you look gorgeous." And then his arms enveloped her, and they looked like one dark shadow. A moment later, I realized they were kissing.

My eyebrows raised. Okay, then. Apparently, they'd skipped right past the friend stage and now were full steam ahead.

Although, technically, they were still married. All those years, both of them had waited.

I leaned back in the swing, thankful I'd trusted my gut not to follow her out there. I watched my parents embrace for the first time in my life. Talk about surprises. I could have never predicted this. Were we actually a family again? I shook my head. This was all too much.

Then it registered that it didn't matter what I thought. They deserved to be happy, the same as me. And I realized life was weird, and I've never gotten used to it. Maybe that was the perfect place to be. Who knew what tomorrow might bring? I didn't always have to prepare for the worst. Life proved anything wonderful could be just around the corner.

2 8

AFTERWORD

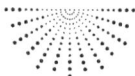

Thank you for reading! Check out the next adventure in the Flamingo mystery series, Selling Sabotage.

And while you are waiting, maybe the Secret Library Cozy Mysteries will whet your appetite.

Made in the USA
Monee, IL
08 November 2024